MAX VALENTINE IS LOOKING AT ME!

HART SISTERS: BOOK THREE

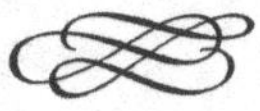

ALIE GARNETT

Copyright © 2020 by Alie Garnett

All rights reserved.

No part of this book may be reproduced in any form or by any electronic or mechanical means, including information storage and retrieval systems, without written permission from the author, except for the use of brief quotations in a book review.

This book is a work of fiction. Names, Characters, places and incidents either are products of the authors wild imagination or are used fictitiously. Any resemblance to actual events or locals or persons, living or dead is entirely coincidental.

Edited by Thoth Editing

Image © DepositPhotos – dashek

Cover Design © Designed with Grace

❧ Created with Vellum

For M & G.

CHAPTER 1

THE WHISKEY BURNED as it went down Della's throat, but it was the burn that made it so satisfying. The burn was supposed to dull the pain of her messed-up life, and what a mess it was.

Twenty-four hours ago, Della Connor Hart had just been invited to be the newest partner at Rodgers and Associates, the law firm she had been at for a decade. According to her life plan, she would've gotten the position earlier than expected. Partner by thirty-five? Check and mate, baby. In less than a day, she'd been reduced to a washed-up lawyer. That checklist of hers? It was in tatters and would never be needed again:

1. graduate from high school early: check
2. make it through undergrad early: check
3. graduate top of the class from law school: check
4. get a job at a renowned firm: check
5. make partner by thirty-five: un-checked
6. judge by fifty: never going to happen

Della was already thirty-three and would not make it that high again, much less in two years. Honestly, she didn't think she'd ever make it that high again in this lifetime. She had been fired today without being given a recommendation letter. Without that, her chances of getting another job in corporate law was practically zero. Her career was in the toilet. That's why she was drinking tonight.

After Della waved at the bartender for another shot, she looked at the empty glass in front of her, wondering if she was pushing herself too far. Being only an inch over five feet and one hundred ten pounds soaking wet, she had never been able to hold her liquor. Actually, she had spent most of her life avoiding the stuff. But today? Today was for getting wasted.

Earlier this afternoon, she had stood in the center of a conference room before Milton Rodgers and nineteen partners and was told she was fired due to violating their office code of ethics. Specifically, she was being let go because she had slept with a coworker who was a married man. That was a big no-no in the company, though it had happened before, and she had not found a single case where anyone had been fired for it. Not that she could bring that up since they didn't even let her defend herself against the accusation. If given a chance, she probably would've won the argument; she was a good lawyer. But Milton's son-in-law, Grant Miller, had lied saying she had been sleeping with him. Which wasn't true, and they had no proof, but she had not been able to say anything in her defense.

If she had, she would have told them that Grant had run to Milton Rodgers before she could report him for taking credit for her work. He had been stealing her cases just as she was getting done with them. He had been changing her name on filing documents for months. It had taken her a long time to notice, but once she did last week, she had been unable to talk to Milton before Grant had thrown her career in the trash can. He was a partner and had been sitting there smirking as she lost everything she had worked for. Oddly, he wasn't fired for the same offense as her.

Della groaned as she looked into the mirror behind the bar. She still looked great. She had bought a new suit in navy blue for her promotion. Navy blue was her color, and the skirt and blazer cost more than she should've spent on it, but it had fit like a glove. It brought out the flecks of blue in her green eyes and made her ass look awesome. She had added a green blouse for a little luck. Though she couldn't see them right now, her designer five-inch heels in matching navy were amazing … and amazingly expensive.

Her mouse brown hair was pulled back in a tight bun, her usual hairstyle for work. It was prim and proper for a successful lawyer. Using the mirror, she pulled the pins that held her hair up, and her hair came raining down just past her shoulders. She ran her fingers through the dark strands, shaking out the ends. The face looking back at her was suddenly surrounded by chocolate brown hair that was straight and had no body to it at all. Was that really her? Della Hart?

Della was actually a red head with natural curls that men and women spent big money to get. Meanwhile, she'd spent her money to control it. She had a standing appointment with Rachel every two weeks. Color and straightening were done on a schedule. One of her only female law professors had told her that good lawyers were not red heads. Taking that to heart, Della went that day to the salon and never looked back. She had embraced the color changes over the years, going from blond to brunette and raven-black, and everything in between. Except for shades of red. Never even a highlight.

When the whiskey arrived, she pulled off her glasses she threw them into the empty shot glass. "You can have those. I won't need them anymore."

"You look great without them," the bartender said as he took the glasses away.

Watching him walk away, she almost called him back, but she knew she really didn't need them. Even though she had been blessed with perfect vision, Della had started to wear the glasses when she'd started at Rodgers and Associates. It had been a disguise she had worn when she had started the job at twenty-two, and all of her coworkers were at least three years older than her. Most people hadn't even graduated from college when she'd started her law career. Glasses made her look and feel older, so she fit in a little better at work. At thirty-three, she didn't need any help with that.

Della watched the golden liquid swirl as she spun the glass, not noticing the man standing next to the barstool beside her. She was so focused on the whiskey in front of her that she almost yelped in surprise when he said her name.

"DC?" Max Valentine said the name she had always went by at work. She had left Della behind after graduating from law school, but now embraced it in every way but work. There she had remained DC, and sometimes just Dee.

Della slowly set the glass down as she answered, "Leave me alone, Max Valentine."

"We need to talk." He pulled out the chair beside her.

"We have nothing to talk about. I've been fired. You were there, Valentine. You saw what happened."

Movement in the mirror caught her attention, and she watched him sit down beside her. His dark hair was cut short and was the color of melted chocolate. She had noticed it the first day she had met him over ten years ago, and her name association for him had been his hair. Valentine chocolates equaled Max Valentine. She never forgot his name, even his first name, which was Maximillian. His gray eyes met hers through the mirror. He had caught her looking.

"How did you find me?" Her tone was demanding. It wasn't like they ran in the same circles. Of course, she had never been in this bar before; it wasn't her kind of place. But for all she knew, he came here every day.

"Your car was in the parking lot at work still, so I started checking the nearby bars. I lucked out and found you." He caught the bartender's eyes and ordered a whiskey as well.

"You win, you found me. Now you can leave." She picked up the glass in front of her.

"You shouldn't have been fired," Max said beside her.

Her head popped up, and she narrowed her eyes at him. "Nice of you to say that here." She swept the nearly empty room with her arm. "You could've said that back there, where it would have helped."

Max was one of the newer partners, but he had still been there in the room with everyone else, judging her and not letting her defend herself.

"I never really thought it would get that bad. I thought someone else would say something," Max explained.

"Who, Valentine? Who? You were supposed to be my friend. I've known you for ten years. I thought we were friends." She ended on a near whisper.

"We were friends. We are friends." His words fell on deaf ears. She wasn't listening to him.

"I'm starting to realize that I had no true friends in that place." She admitted it more to herself than him.

Watching him in the mirror, he pulled a piece of paper from his coat pocket and laid it next to her. Della glanced down; it only contained a phone number. She left the paper where it was and said, "Not interested, Max. You can keep your number. If I had wanted to screw you, I would have by now."

Which was a lie, and she knew it. She would've screwed him any day, anytime if he had only asked. Max Valentine didn't even know she existed most of the time they had worked together. Over the years, she had noticed he was the office playboy, but she was never the benefactor of his attention.

He laughed as if she had said a joke. "That's not my number. It's a friend's number. He has a job for you."

"I can get my own job," she stated, but she knew she would have difficulties with that project. But in no way was she getting help from him.

"We both know you'll have trouble with that." Apparently, Max knew it too.

"Not interested." She pushed the paper back in front of him.

"It's with the government."

"Do I get to be a spy? Is this how you get to be a spy? I might want to be a spy," she asked, looking around the room for other spies. He was being so vague about what he was offering. It was the only thing that made sense.

"No." He laughed again. This time she smiled a little as well. "John works for the DA. He's always looking for good lawyers."

"Why don't you work for him?"

Max shrugged. "I don't want to be in the government."

"Me either."

"You have no prospects. John will hire you on just a word from me." He took a drink of his whiskey.

"I can find myself a job." Della insisted, though she knew it was going to be almost impossible.

"I'll call him tonight and tell him to expect to hear from you," Max said, looking in the mirror at her.

"He'll just hire me because you say so? You seem pretty sure of yourself." She swirled her glass again.

They were in the middle of an unspoken standoff. Della had no idea why she wouldn't just take the number, but she had picked her side, and she didn't switch sides in arguments. That's what made her a good lawyer, a great lawyer.

As she ignored Max, who was still sitting beside her, he asked, "Where are your glasses?"

"That nice guy behind the bar took them. He said I look better without them," she answered and waved at the guy as he walked past them. The bartender didn't notice her this time.

"He's right. I never realized you had green eyes," Max replied as he looked at her in the mirror curiously.

"The whole time, friend. The whole time." Della swiveled her chair towards him, setting her glass down as she did. "I guess our friendship never got to that level. Hopefully, you at least know my boob size since you weren't looking at my eyes."

Sliding off the barstool, she grabbed her jacket off the back. "Your's are gray like the clouds during a summer thunderstorm. Sometimes, when you're wearing blue, they turn blueish gray. I did consider you my friend."

He blinked at her words. "Take the number, Della. You're exactly what he's looking for." He pushed the paper with the number on it in her hand. She sighed and shoved the paper in her pocket, but she wasn't going to call. She didn't need his help.

Turning towards the door, she made a dramatic exit, stiff back and chin up. Ten steps in, she realized she had forgotten her phone on the bar, so she had to turn around and go get it. Just her luck.

Max was holding it up when she walked back, a grin on his face. As she grabbed it from him, it went off. It was Zoey's ringtone chorus from the song "Queen of Hearts." Her younger sister had programmed it into Della's phone, and she had yet to change it. She loved the song, and it made her happy when her baby sister called. Usually.

Still grinning, Max didn't let go of her phone. She stopped trying to take it from his hand but shut the ringer off and the song stopped.

"Is it your husband?" Gray eyes locked on hers.

"I don't have a husband." She held the stare. With two younger sisters, she was usually able to win a staring contest without much effort. Many long years of practice.

He looked surprised but held her gaze. "I thought you were married?"

"Why?" she asked, not looking away. What had made him think she was married?

"You changed your name a few years ago."

"You're right, I did. I guess I forgot." She'd completely locked in on those gray orbs. She could've stared at them all day.

A few years ago, she had added Connor to her last name after her father had died. Connor was her middle name. Both her and Zoey were Connor Harts now, and their middle sister, Evie, had married young and had kept her husband's last name.

"You forgot you changed your name?" he said in disbelief.

"I had been planning it a long time before I did it." It was her only explanation. It was the truth, and since she had only moved her middle name to join her last name, it really wasn't a big deal. Delphinea Connor Hart changed to Delphinea Connor Hart; no real change. But nobody ever called her Delphinea; she had always been Della to family and friends. Her professional name had changed the most, going from DC Hart to D Connor Hart.

She finally pulled the phone from his hand and said, "Some days, the queen doesn't take the hand. Today was one of those days. Good-bye, Max Valentine. Have a nice life." After breaking eye contact, she was finally able to make her dramatic exit.

CHAPTER 2

SARAH WAS DRIVING HIM CRAZY. "Let's go to the farmer's market and poke around for a while," she had said, then she kept disappearing on him once they got here. This was not Max Valentine's usual scene, but he had a book to avoid writing and a little sister who wanted to spend time with him.

He had been researching for his book for six months now; he had to start writing it. But every time he sat to write, he'd found something else to do. Anything else, from organizing his research again to surfing the internet. He was even calling his mom and dad more frequently.

So, here he was, avoiding his computer and looking at a sea of tomatoes, wondering if these people really thought they would sell them all. Every stand had hundreds of them, all in different colors and sizes. Their prices were all the same, and he was lost in the land of tomatoes.

Summer had officially hit Minneapolis, and it was hot. He was starting to think that the shorts and T-shirt he wore was being over-dressed for the day. It was just after noon, and the sun was relentless overhead. Max stopped to look at some tomatoes, just to stand under the protective canopies overhead. He enjoyed being out of the sun.

As he was looking at the booth's tomatoes, he started wondering if he should bring any home. Max immediately scrunched his nose and wondered where the thought came from—he barely liked tomatoes. That's when he heard it, a voice he recognized but couldn't place. So, he listened in hopes the name would come to him as the voice went on.

"I know, Mrs. Willis, cherry for the salads. I know what you like." The voice laughed as she talked to an older lady. Max looked up and saw a redhead who didn't look familiar to him at all.

Before he could figure out who she was, she was standing in front of him, asking, "Are you buying anything, Max?"

When his name left her lips, she slammed her eyes shut. When they opened again, green eyes stared back at him, green eyes that had been on his mind for the last eight months. Recognition hit him hard. It was DC Connor Hart, and she had changed. The last time he saw her was at the bar in downtown Minneapolis after she'd been fired. He had given her John's number to call, and she hadn't. He'd checked.

Her hair was still shoulder length but now red and more curly then wavy. She was wearing a tight-fitting green T-shirt that said "Hart Farms." He had never seen her in a T-shirt, much less a tight one.

"Hello, DC. It's been a while. How have you been?" Max was happy to see her again, and he liked the change.

"Good. Are you buying anything? I'm busy," she said, clearly annoyed.

Smiling, he blindly reached over and grabbed a random box of what he assumed were tomatoes. "These."

"Okay, five dollars." She put the box in a paper bag.

Reaching into his pocket, he pulled out a ten-dollar bill and gave it to her. "I want to talk to you."

"No, thank you. Thanks for shopping." She gave him his change and dismissed him.

As Della turned away from him, he caught a glimpse of her perfect butt in tight red leggings. Everything about her outfit was form-fitting, and man, what a form it fit. How had she hidden those curves for ten years? Better yet, *why* had she hidden them?

"Della, go eat so you can talk to the guy," said a sandy-haired man, who was also in the stand with her. Max hadn't noticed him until he spoke; his eyes had been stuck on Della. He wondered if she was really a redhead. He couldn't remember her ever having red hair before.

"I'll eat, but I don't need to talk. Call if you need me, Gabe." She didn't glance his way as she walked out the back of the booth. Max grabbed his sack of tomatoes and followed her. From this view, he could watch the red leggings cradle her round butt perfectly. On her feet were strappy four-inch heeled sandals. "DC, I want to talk to you."

Della turned and planted her hands on her hips. Her green eyes seemed to spark as she said, "We have nothing to talk about. I thought you had left. Where's your girlfriend?"

"Sarah? So, you saw us earlier?" He wanted to explain that Sarah was his sister, but he didn't. Had Della recognized him right away? Or had it taken a while like it had for him?

"Yes, Sarah. Go talk to her. She's your girlfriend, so she probably wants to talk to you. I don't, remember? We're not friends." Della turned on her heel and left, and he followed her again.

All he had to do was watch that exquisite hind-end, and she would stop eventually. Her first stop was at a hamburger stand, where the line was ten people deep. She went up to the area where you pick up the order and yelled, "Hank, I need a burger!"

The cook leaned back and looked at her with a smile, "Onions, Dell?"

"God, no. Just cheese, two slices." She yelled back at the man, holding up two fingers.

Suddenly, she whipped around and glared at Max. "Stop following me or I'll report you to the cops."

Max rolled his eyes. "I just want to talk for a second."

"The guy I left in the booth is a cop. I can have you arrested in a heartbeat."

Had she always been this sassy? Had he never noticed before?

The man on the grill walked over with a paper plate and handed it to her. "This guy bothering you, Della?"

"No, Hank. He's leaving right now." She dropped some pickles on her burger and walked away from the stand.

Max pointed at an empty picnic table. "Can we just sit? You just eat, and I'll talk. Then I'll leave you alone forever."

"Forever? Is that a promise?" She sat down at the table and took a big bite from the burger. He could tell she didn't care how she looked; she was hungry.

"You didn't pay for that," Max observed as he sat, putting his bag of tomatoes between them.

"Hank gets all his onions from Hart Farms, so we get free burgers. It's called a contract, Valentine. Maybe you've heard about those?" She took another bite and smirked.

As he watched her, he noticed she was way more relaxed than he'd ever seen her. At the office, she been seriously uptight. This woman was completely different. She was making jokes.

"Why didn't you call John? He told me you never called," Max asked.

"For a while, I thought it was a joke. Why would you try and help me? Then I had moved on," she said cryptically.

"You sell vegetables at the farmer's market?" He looked around.

"So what if I do? I can do whatever I want to do." She opened his bag and grabbed a handful of tiny tomatoes, then popped one in her mouth. "Love these."

"You can, but you were a great lawyer." He knew she was the best the firm had … until they fired her.

"I'm a great lawyer. You let them fire me, for what? For sleeping with Grant? As if I'd throw away my career for him." She took another bite of the burger.

"Max!" Sarah ran up to him, breathless. "I found you. I have to go; work called."

Sarah breezed in like always. Tall, blonde, and breathless was how people described his baby sister. Without a word, he pulled his car keys out his pocket, and she grabbed them. Sarah kissed him on the forehead and was gone.

"Now you're carless." DC looked at him flatly as she popped another tomato into her mouth. Max watched her smirking at him as she ate. He wondered if she knew how sexy she looked doing that.

"I'll get a ride. I'm not far anyway." He was enjoying just watching her eat.

"Quit watching me eat. I haven't had anything since 5:00 a.m. I deserve to eat unwatched. Is it hard to watch a woman eat since your girlfriend doesn't?" She took another bite.

"Everybody calls you Della here. Is that what the D stands for?" He dismissed her comment about his girlfriends. He really had no idea what she was talking about.

"Yes, Max Valentine. I was going through a phase when I started at the firm, but now I'm over it," she explained.

He smiled at her. She'd rarely called him anything but Valentine. "You can just call me just Max. How long have you worked at your stand?"

"Since eight this morning. It's been a long day."

"Nice dodge, Della," he used her name, and it felt better than saying DC. "Years?"

"They're called seasons. This is number seven, I guess," she said, taking another handful of tomatoes from his bag.

"You were working here when you were at the law firm? It is against the rules to have another job." He knew the rules just as well as she did.

Grinning, Della reached for more tomatoes as she asked, "Are you going to get me fired, Valentine? Are you going to tell on me? At least then it would've been true."

"Is that why you never went on the weekend retreats?" he questioned. Every month, the younger lawyers at the firm would get together and go weekend trips. Mostly, it was just an excuse to drink and hook up, and nobody got fired for those.

"Yes and no. I didn't want to go on those weird trips. I'm not a big partier, and weekends were the only time I could see my family. But I did help my sister at the farmer's markets on the weekends. She never paid me with money, so it wasn't income, just food." She winked at him, then held up a tiny tomato before popping it into her mouth.

"So, it's not your booth?" He was having a hard time imagining her doing this in her tailored skirts and stilettos, but then his mind flashed to the tight pants and heels she was now wearing at a farmer's market.

Della looked up at him. "No, I don't do the vegetable thing. My sisters do, though. I opened my own family law firm in my hometown."

So, she had landed on her feet. Until she'd said it, he hadn't realized how worried he had been about her. "Congratulations. Your own firm? That's awesome!"

"It's just me, so it's not really impressive. How is it at the office?"

Did she blush a little at his compliment? He leaned back and said, "Couldn't say. I quit just after Christmas."

"Why? You were a partner. You had made it!" Her eyes lit up as she talked. If he thought she'd looked good at the bar months ago, she was radiant now.

"I felt like they had been asses to you. You were the best lawyer there, Della. You were the one everyone went to when they had questions, even the partners," he replied.

"Where are you now?" she asked.

"I'm actually taking time off to write a book." He didn't like talking about it anymore, thanks to a tremendous case of writer's block. After months of research, he needed to start, but he had no idea how.

She ate the last tomato on her plate as her phone indicated she had received a text. Pulling it out of her pocket, she chewed as she read. Her eyes widened, and she jumped up. "I have to go. Have a nice life, Max Valentine." And she was off, hurrying through the crowd in her leggings and heels.

He took her empty plate and grabbed his bag, which was also empty, and threw them away. Della had eaten all his tomatoes. Maybe he would stop by and buy some more since he would have to walk home anyway.

As her stand came into view, he noticed the cop was gone, and it was just her. The crowd was still gathered around the booths. As she talked, she organized the vegetables into straighter lines. *Multitasking. That's the Della I know*, Max thought to himself.

His phone rang, and he glanced at it. His mother was calling. With a sigh, he answered the phone and turned to leave the farmer's market. Maybe he would stop by again next week and see if he could learn anything more about this woman. He had worked with her for ten years and suddenly found her fascinating.

CHAPTER 3

WITH RELIEF, Della watched as Max Valentine walked away, talking on his phone. He looked just as good coming as he did going. Della always liked the way he walked.

It was no surprise that he hadn't noticed her until they were practically face to face. Meanwhile, she'd noticed him walking around an hour ago. He had never really noticed her at work, either. They had actually started on the same day, and by the time orientation was over, she'd known his name and what colleges he'd attended. He had first called her by her name almost a year later. Della assumed it never crossed his mind to learn it.

Maybe he would've learned her name faster if she'd gone on those stupid party retreats with her coworkers, but she hated partying, and during her first years at the firm, her sister had ended up pregnant and widowed. Not long after that, her youngest sister was running wild. She had spent every weekend trying to help her dad deal with things two hours away in Birch Cove. Since her mother had run off a decade before with another guy, Della was the only one who could help.

After she had left the firm, she realized nobody really noticed her there. She had actually worked with close to one hundred fifty people, and she hadn't talked to any of them since she walked out the door.

14

Nor did any of them reach out to her. Except Max, first at the bar, and now here. But Max Valentine was not a friend.

Looking back, it had been her fault. She kept everyone at arm's length, never letting anyone get close. She'd always been uncomfortable at the large law firm; it was intimidating. But then again, she was twenty-two when she'd started, and not as mature as her fellow workers. She had pushed through her fear and had succeeded and thrived on the work, although she had never gotten comfortable with the people.

After she had left and started her own firm, her comfort level had skyrocketed. Della knew almost every woman who came in the doors looking for a lawyer. She mostly worked with women, and the county hadn't treated these women fairly for years. The judges were set in their ways, and it seemed that the local lawyers didn't approve of divorce for any reason, even when they represented the women in court.

Driving into Birch Cove on that late October afternoon, she had stopped at the house she had inherited from her grandparents, and she felt at home. It was actually a mansion, and it was dirty, dusty, and in need of repairs before she could use it, but it was hers, and she loved it immediately.

Repairs and cleaning should have taken months, but most of the work had been done in less than two. Her sister Zoey had insisted she wanted to be married in the house at Christmas. With that in mind, the entire family had chipped in to help, and by Christmas, the house was shining like the jewel it used to be—at least on the inside. This summer, her carpenter, Chad, would be working on the exterior painting and repairs. He'd started earlier this week.

Since she had opened the doors in January, she'd had no shortage of clients. In fact, she had too many, but she couldn't say no to these women. Each woman she talked to had a story to tell about how their last lawyer hadn't even tried, or worse, been on their ex's side. There were two lawyers in town. Both of them were over fifty, and both were men who shouldn't have be allowed to practice law at all.

With so many clients, she was in court at least once a week, and sometimes twice. She should have spent today at home, working on filings for the four cases she was working on. She worked longer hours now than at her old firm, but the upside was that since she worked from home, she could sit on the couch in her PJs, binge-watching TV and working at the same time.

Yesterday she had told her sister Evie that she could only give her one day this weekend; Evie and Zoey had to figure it out after that. Della pushed her sister to hire some teenagers for the summer. There was no way her sisters would be able to do it all on their own this year.

Della smiled as she handed a bag to a man and thought about the fact that both of her sisters had had babies last month. Right at the peak of the farmer's market season too. Their husbands, and Evie's son, Ben, had been helping out way more than they should, just so Zoey and Evie could take it easy.

In just the last year, their family had quickly expanded, with both of her sisters marrying between Thanksgiving and Christmas, and then having babies a month apart. Last year it had been the three sisters and one nephew, and now the family had exploded.

It had taken Della time to adjust to the new men in her sisters' lives. They were now all lovey-dovey, and somedays, Della couldn't handle it. She felt out of place amongst the couples. Other days she loved that her sisters were finally as happy as they deserved to be.

Maybe she was a little jealous of her little sisters finding men who loved them so much, but Della knew there was no man out there for her. She had realized that years ago.

CHAPTER 4

LOOKING up at the plum-colored Victorian, Max knew his mother owed him big time for this. He hadn't been five minutes and was already dreading spending the next few weeks in this house.

Opening the car door, he climbed out into the mid-June heat of Birch Cove, Minnesota. He could hear a lawnmower in the distance; he could even smell the cut grass. Summer was in full bloom.

This was where he was going to write a book, where there were no distractions. All he could do was get over this wall and write his book.

Three days ago, he was staring at his computer when his mother, Elizabeth, had called. She had asked if he wanted some help with meals so he could write without distractions. He had thought she was going to hire someone to help him; instead, she'd said to go spend time with her aunts in Birch Cove and that they would love to cook his meals.

Knowing he would say no to the offer, she'd added that Sally had been having dizzy spells, and she wanted someone in the family to go check and make sure Sally was okay. Since Max wasn't working anymore, he should be that person. That was code for "Since you're not doing anything anyway."

So here he was, walking up to the front door of Sally and Mae Neilson, sisters in their eighties who'd never married or had children and had lived together forever. They had come to some holidays when he was growing up, but he hadn't seen them in a few years. Now he was going to spend a month in their house.

Once he had made it up the steps, he heard a voice from beside him say, "You made it, Maxy." He knew it was Sally. She'd liked calling him that since he was little.

Turning, he found her sitting on the front porch swing, wearing a long pants and a long-sleeved shirt. The heat was obviously not affecting her. "Hello, Sally, were you waiting for me?"

She chuckled. "No."

Not knowing what that meant, he let it go. "Are you coming inside?"

"No, but you can sit with me if you want for a while." She patted the seat beside her.

He had nothing better to do and didn't want to leave the old lady sitting alone in the heat, so he sat next to her and instantly wished he'd gone inside to the air-conditioning. "How are you doing?"

"I'm great. No complaints." She sounded good, better than he'd expected after talking to his mother. "I hear you're writing a book."

He was always happy to talk about the book, less happy when it came to typing it. "That's why I'm here. No interruptions in Birch Cove."

She sat up straighter, and he wondered if he had offended her by saying nothing happened in this town. Then he saw the lawnmower he had been hearing come around the giant house in front of them across the street. A young man in his mid-twenties was pushing the mower, only wearing shorts and tennis shoes. No shirt. He brought the mower to the curb and shut it off, then pushed it to the garage on the side of the house.

When he disappeared into the garage, Sally said in a loud whisper, "Isn't he fine?"

Max just stared at her for a moment, then replied, "He's not really my type." Then the young man came out of the garage and went into the house. Within moments, he was back out of the house and about to open the door to his old truck when he called out, "Hi, Miss Sally."

His aunt stood up, waving energetically. "Hi, Chad."

Chad replied, "Say hi to Miss Mae for me."

"I will. Are you coming back tomorrow?" his aunt asked casually.

"Yes, I have to paint." Then he got in his truck and drove off.

Once his truck disappeared down the road, Sally said, "What are we doing out in this heat? Let's go inside."

Max was at a loss for words. He looked down at the little old lady beside him, who'd apparently been waiting for the young neighbor man to finish mowing the lawn. Maybe it wouldn't be as boring around here as he thought it was going to be.

Following Sally into the house, he was surprised to see the house hadn't changed since he was last here, which was when he'd been eleven. The furniture was the same, the paint was the same, even the warm feeling was still the same. The house was trapped in the forties or before, he couldn't pinpoint a date.

The other thing that immediately struck him was the heat. It was hotter in here than it was outside. How was he going to live like this?

Mae walked into the entry from the living room area as Max and Sally were coming into the house. She was taller and skinnier than Sally's short plumpness. They were complete opposite in looks, but he was glad to see Mae still looked like his grandfather, who had passed away while Max was in law school. He liked the reminder of the old man.

"Maxy made it," Sally announced.

"He's just in time for tea," Mae answered and turned to go back to the dining room. Both Max and Sally obediently followed.

Sally sat in what seemed to be her usual spot across from Mae and patted the seat between the two for Max. He sat and took a cookie from the plate in front of him. There was no way he would be unable to drink hot tea in the furnace.

"Chad said hi today." Sally sounded like a schoolgirl with her first crush.

"He says hi every day," Mae said flatly.

"He was mowing the lawn today. Tomorrow he's painting again." Sally seemed proud that she knew the young man's plans.

Mae made a grunting noise across the table.

"I didn't see Delly today, but she was there. The door wasn't locked." Sally didn't take the cue that Mae wasn't interested.

"She was probably working. It is in the middle of the day." She shrugged, then turned to Max. "She's a lawyer like you."

"I don't practice law anymore."

Sally took his hand. "I thought you have been a lawyer for years. Do you still need to practice?"

"Sally, that's just what they say: practicing law, practicing medicine," Mae chided Sally, probably a little too harshly. "Delphinea is having Chad fix up the old Connor Mansion, and she's practicing out of there. Chad's taking his own sweet time too."

"There's a lot to do, Mae." Sally defended the carpenter.

"He's taking advantage, Sally. I was there at the wedding, and most of the main floor was done. I heard the entire upstairs is already fixed up," Mae argued.

"Mae, you saw all that woodwork that was painted! He has to take it down, get the paint off, stain it again, then put it back up. That's a lot of work. Delly told me herself. And now he has to paint the outside. It's going to take all summer." Sally smiled, showing off she had the inside scoop.

"He usually only works a few hours and then leaves," Mae pointed out.

"He's busy," Sally replied flatly, then turned to Max to explain. "He's in a band, and his girlfriend just had twins. He has a lot on his plate right now."

Max whistled low and said, "In a band, huh?"

"It's a rock-n-roll band," Sally told him with a shy grin.

"It is not. He didn't play rock-n-roll at the wedding." Mae folded her arms over her chest.

"Yes, he did," Sally insisted.

Mae shook her head. "No."

"Yes, you just don't know what rock-n-roll is anymore. Your too old to understand," Sally shot back.

Max was having the time of his life. These two would make staying in Birch Cove way more fun than staying in Minneapolis. Mae had no comeback for the "old" comment. Max wondered if they fought like this all the time, or just when they had company.

"You, Sally love, are only two years older than me. Two." Mae got up, taking her plate, his plate, and her cup, and walked out of the room.

Sally leaned back in her chair and laughed. "She hates to lose an argument."

"Do you argue a lot?" Max asked, suppressing a grin.

She nodded. "Most every day, but it makes our relationship stronger."

He looked at his great aunt and thought she had said the most profound thing he had ever heard. He realized they each knew what page the other was on all the time; no surprises. Maybe he would try it with his next relationship and see if it worked.

"What did you think of Chad?" Sally asked. Max wondered if she had memory problems. She had already asked.

"I really didn't get a good look at him, but I don't think he was my type," Max admitted.

Sally laughed. "That's right. You should see Delly; she's adorable."

Max was about to say he wasn't looking for a relationship when Mae injected, "Her *sister* is adorable, Sally. Delphinea is *fetching*."

"Mae's right, but Delly's more delightful then fetching." Sally agreed.

"Don't try your little games, Sally. Max isn't interested in Delphinea. He doesn't even know her. Maybe if he knew her, he would be," Mae said to her sister.

Max stood up, ending the conversation about the neighbor, and said, "I think I'll go get the rest of my stuff and start unpacking."

Mae followed him to the entry and explained. "I put you in the front bedroom with the turret. You always liked that room when you were little. The bath across the hall is all yours."

He hurried out of the house and hoped he wouldn't run into the delightful Delphinea. There was no way he was interested in dating while he was here. He was only thinking about getting this book written, then maybe he would swing by the farmer's market and see if Della Connor Hart was still angry at him. Maybe with time, she'd stop blaming him for something he really had no control over.

CHAPTER 5

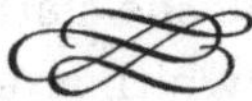

DELLA SURVEYED her freshly mowed lawn as she approached her house after another bad day in court. Another woman in this county had lost full custody of her kids to an abusive husband. Judge Cramer knew Mike Kelley from the multiple times he had been in that very courtroom for other offenses: bar fights, break-ins, you name it. And still, the judge said those two little girls deserve to spend more time with him, even though he never showed up for the times he could've had them before.

It was hard to be a good lawyer in a town where the judges sucked, but at least she didn't have to mow the lawn. If her sisters weren't so busy on the farm, she would've had her nephew mow it; he was twelve now. But with everything going on out there with all the babies, it was easier just to pay her carpenter to do it. Chad was high-priced, but he also did a good job.

It was hot today, and she was glad she had worn her black pencil skirt and thin lavender button-up sleeveless blouse from her past life as a big-city lawyer. It was late in the day, and she had nothing on her plate for the rest of the evening except paperwork, but she could do that in her upstairs office in her pajamas.

Looking up at the window of her office upstairs, she smiled. It was very different than her office in the city. There was a small desk in the corner, and the center of the room had a large oversized couch, where she did most of her work. The TV was usually on when she was in there. She loved her upstairs office, and her other office downstairs was great too. It had the big desk she had always dreamed of having, and she worked there during the day.

Turning down her sidewalk, she started up the stairs when a loud crash behind her made her whirl around. There, standing in the middle of Maple Street, was Max Valentine, holding a box that had opened from the bottom. All the books it had held were in the street.

"Max Valentine. Are you stalking me?" she asked, setting down her briefcase on the sidewalk.

"No, I swear." He dropped the empty box to the ground, clearly shocked as well. "I'm staying with my aunts for a while to work on my book."

"I forgot about your book." She lied as she walked towards him. She'd never forgotten anything about Max Valentine. Della was glad she'd worn her five-inch heels today, because he was tall, and she hated being so short. A bonus was that she knew that they made her legs look great. *Take that, Max Valentine,* she thought to herself.

"I'm still working on it." He bent down and started to stack the books and papers into piles.

"I assume so. I only talked to you two weeks ago." After walking over to him, she started picking up the papers that had scattered.

"Do you live there?" he asked, pointing to the mansion behind her.

She turned and looked at it like it was the first time she had seen it. It really needed some fresh paint, but the shingles were now new, and the shrubs were a little more tamed. She still loved it. "Yes, I live there."

"It's a big house," he said.

"No, it's a mansion. It's the Connor Mansion, and I live and work there." She was proud of what she had accomplished in such a short time.

"Wait. You're Delly? Delphinea?" he asked in disbelief.

"Sally and Mae. I bet you're Maxy and Maximillian." She smiled and put the papers she had gathered on his pile.

How had she not known he was their nephew? In the last few months, she had learned everything about the two women. They had been a staple in town for generations. But never had one mentioned Max Valentine. That she would've remembered.

"Have they talked about me?" he asked, his papers and books now in two piles.

"No, Sally gives everyone a nickname, and Mae always calls people by their given name. Except for Sally," she replied.

He looked up at her and asked, "Sally isn't Sally?"

She laughed. "Sally's real name is Patricia. You're staying with them, Valentine. You should know these things."

He picked up a pile of books. "I guess you know them better than I do."

Looking at the other pile, she decided she'd better help him out, or someone would drive over the books. Della picked up the other pile and gestured at their sidewalk. "Lead the way."

"You don't have to help," he said as he turned and walked towards the house.

Following behind him, she admired his backside. Today, he was in cargo shorts and an orange T-shirt. It should've look awful with his brown hair, but it looked amazing on him.

He opened the door for her with one hand, then followed her into the house. She said hello to the women that were reading in the living room as they walked through. Della hadn't been over as much as during the winter and spring. How the women lived without an air conditioner, she didn't know.

"Upstairs in the turret room, Delphinea. You know the one." Mae waved at the stairs.

Della knew the room, but not the directions. The turret room was in the front of the house, directly across from her upstairs office. She had been in every room on the main floor when she came over to visit the older women to make sure they were okay. Sometimes, she'd make Chad check on them when she was busy. Sally liked having Chad talk to her, so he was a good choice.

When she made it to the top of the stairs, she walked into the room. Della put the books on the bed and went to looked out the panoramic windows of the turret. From her vantage point, she had a clear view into her house.

"So, how are you related to the Neilson's?" She turned as he was putting his books down.

"My mom's father was their brother."

"Their brother?"

Max nodded. "He died while I was in college."

"Okay." She would let it drop. If he didn't know about the older ladies, she wasn't going to tell him. "How are you going to work in this heat, Max Valentine?"

"I don't know. I'll have to open windows, probably. Maybe buy myself a little window air conditioner," he said.

She pulled her shirt away from her skin; it was stifling in the room. She saw his eyes shift to the front of her shirt. Dropping her hands immediately, she crossed her arms. "Good luck with that. Mae will never let you use her electricity like that. You are so wasteful, Max Valentine."

"Then maybe I'll have to go across the road and find a corner in that mansion of yours. I bet it's like a freezer in there." He looked past her at the house on the other side of the street.

"You bet it is. I don't like being hot." Their eyes met from across the room.

"Seems you're pretty comfortable with being hot, Delphinea." He smiled with his eyes, holding hers like he did at the bar months before.

Her breath caught, was he flirting with her? Max Valentine, flirting with her. Her mind started going places it shouldn't have. Shaking her head, she dismissed the thought and said, "Don't call me that. It's Della."

He took a step closer to her, his brown eyes boring into hers, and replied, "Once you call me Max and not Max Valentine."

"Okay. Max it is." She conceded. Now it was time to go. It was getting weird in here, in his bedroom. "Only Mae gets to call me the other."

As she walked past him, he lightly grabbed her hand. "Why Mae?"

Her attention immediately went to the hand he was holding and the tingles of electricity running up her arm. With more effort than she wanted to admit, she shook his hand off. "Because I was named after her mother."

Then she was out of the room, away from his steamy eyes and electricity.

CHAPTER 6

Sweat was running down his back as he watched Della's sexy rear end walk out of his bedroom. How had he never noticed how nice her butt was? He'd wasted years not watching her walk away from him. It was nearly a hundred degrees in his room, yet she was hotter than that. He realized she had no idea how sexy she was. She knew how good she looked in clothes, and she bought them because they made her look good, but she had no idea how sexy *she* was.

When she had walked up to him in the middle of the street in those high heels, he could barely talk to her. Then she started picking up his papers, and each time she bent over, he could see down her shirt. So, each time she bent over, he saw her lacy bra that perfectly matched the color of her purple shirt. She didn't even notice it was happening.

Once they were in the house, he had the opportunity to follow her up the stairs and had her sweet butt at eye level as they went. By the time they had made it to his room, he had an erection he couldn't hide, but she hadn't even looked. It had taken fierce strength to not go over to the window she was standing in and kiss her. Then she started to play with her shirt, making him want to fling her onto the bed and have his way with her. She didn't even comment when he called her hot.

Flopping down on the bed, Max tried to get his body back under control. Why was it that he'd never noticed this version of Della before? When he'd heard that she and Grant had hooked up, he had wondered what Grant had seen in the woman. Why would Grant throw everything away on her? Now he was one hundred percent sure Grant had never slept with her. Grant wouldn't have been able to handle her in bed. Groaning now, Max rubbed his hands over his face. He had to stop thinking about Della Connor Hart because now he was starting to wonder if he could handle her in bed. Nevertheless, he wanted to give it a try.

He got up and organized his papers a little before heading downstairs when he was sure he was ready to be around people again. The sisters were still in the living room reading, still not caring that it was eight hundred degrees in the house.

Sally lowered her book and asked, "How did you like Delly? She's nice."

He smiled at his aunt and sat on a chair "Yeah, she's nice."

Mae didn't look up but added, "She didn't leave much to the imagination with that outfit."

"Mae, you know how young people are. They like to flaunt it if they got it. Right, Maxy?" Sally said to her sister.

"Sally's right. There was nothing wrong with her outfit," Max said. Nothing at all. It fit perfectly and showed off more of her than he'd ever seen. He liked that.

"It did make her legs look good." Mae nodded, still not looking up from the book.

"That they did." Max agreed with his aunt. These two were an interesting pair.

"It's the shoes. She always wears the tall shoes. She's short," Sally whispered conspiratorially, as if it were a secret.

Max decided the conversation would go on forever with his two great aunts, so it was time to change the subject. Forcing the image out, he asked them, "Della said that she was named after your mom. Is that true?"

Mae finally lowered the book and looked at him. "You didn't know your great-grandmother's name?"

Max had to admit the truth. "No, I had never heard the name Delphinea before."

"I guess you maybe wouldn't have known about her since she has been gone a long time now. Catherine had always loved my mother and asked me if she could name her first baby after her. I told her yes, so little Delphinea has always had a place in my heart. I'm happy she's moved into the mansion." Mae explained, then picked her book back up.

Max leaned back in his chair and thought about Della's dislike for her name. He'd also disliked his own long name. Maybe they have something in common after all—that, and of course, lawyering.

Both sisters were reading again, so he got up without a word to get more stuff from his trunk. If he saw Della again, maybe the bottom of his box wouldn't drop out. She had been the last person he expected to walk down the street in Birch Cove. At first, he had thought he was imagining it, but then she turned around, and he knew it was her.

After hauling the last load of stuff up to the sauna he was calling a bedroom, he took off his shirt to ward off the heat as he organized his stuff. Putting things away, then he set up his laptop and put his books on the bookshelf above the desk. When he got them in order, he grabbed his shirt and wiped the sweat off his face. He went over to the windows to see if they opened any more than they already were … they did not.

His phone dinged with an incoming text. He picked it up and read it:

Unknown: Are you hot?

It was from a number he didn't know, but he gotten text from it three years ago about a merger—a merger he had worked on with Della. Max grinned as he sat on the bed to text her back.

Max: Hot? In this oven. Never.

After he sent the text, he added her name to the number, then went back and changed it to "Queen of Harts," spelling the last word like her last name. Like her ringtone so many months before. It dinged in his hand, and the new name popped up.

Queen of Harts: Nice and cool over here. I think I need a blanket.

Max laughed. She was flirting with him. Did she even realize it?

Max: Maybe you can blow some of that cold air over here.

He waited for her response. He didn't have to wait long.

Queen of Harts: You don't get any of my air.
Max: Selfish

Her response came in quickly this time.

Queen of Harts: I have a fan you can borrow. I'll bring it down, and you can come get it.

Max got up and slid the phone into his pocket. He was getting to see her again.

Nearly running, he bound up her front steps as she opened the door with the fan hanging like a suitcase from her hand. It wasn't the heaven-sent fan that caught his attention, but her soft gray V-neck T-shirt and blue cotton pants. Her curly red hair was now piled on her head in some sort of loose ponytail, but many red strands were sticking out. Sally had been right; she was adorable.

"For me?" he asked, pointing at the fan.

"Yeah, I took pity on you. I remember not having air conditioning. It was miserable." She was still standing in the doorway. He could see she wasn't wearing shoes; her toenails were painted with pink and red stripes. For the first time, he noticed how short she really was. She must have always worn shoes to make herself taller.

Instead of taking the fan from her hands, Max just leaned on the doorframe and said, "Aren't you going to ask me in? It's the neighborly thing to do, you know."

Della grinned and pushed the door open with her back. "Come on in. It's a bit messy. I have to hire someone to take calls, file, and such, but I've been too busy lately."

Max was barely listening as he looked around. Her house was gorgeous. Dark woodwork was everywhere, and off-white walls just made the woodwork more impressive. On the right was a seating area with antique couches and tables, and beyond that, a desk was in the middle of the room with matching file cabinets along the walls. He could see a kitchen in the back of the house, but what caught his attention was the grand staircase in the middle of it all.

He stepped into the house and took the fan from her hands. Della closed the door behind them and leaned against it, watching him.

"This is gorgeous, Della," he said in awe. This is where she got to work?

"Thank you. We've been working on restoring it back to what it was. The interior is just about finished, so now we've got to start working on the outside."

"We?" The word had stopped him cold. He knew she hadn't been married eight months ago, but didn't Sally say something about a wedding in the house?

Della nodded. "My sisters and their husbands, and Chad, of course."

"Do you have the hots for Chad like Sally?"

"Nobody has the hots for Chad like Sally." Della laughed. "He's not my type."

Relief rushed through him. Della wasn't with anyone.

"Seemed like a good-looking young man. Not my type, either. Sally asked twice." He wanted to make her laugh again.

"Sally's always on the lookout for switch-hitters. She tested me when I moved back also." Della smiled and shook her head.

Max turned away from the gorgeous woodwork and looked at her. "She called you adorable."

Della's eyes sparkled as she laughed again. "She didn't; I'm fetching. Only Zoey gets to be called adorable. They talk about us Hart sisters over there?"

Max rested his hand on the doorframe above her head, then leaned into it so he was hovering over her. "You're definitely adorable in this getup."

She pushed his bare chest away from her and walked away from the door, "Quit flirting with me. I must be the only woman within a hundred miles for you to want to do that."

"I'm not flirting with you."

Della raised an eyebrow at him. "Are you just flirting with me to get in my bed? So, you can sleep in air-conditioning?"

"No! Do you really think I'd do that? That I would sleep with you simply for cold air?" He was trying not to shout at her. With his fan, he turned and left the house. At least now he knew what she thought of him. It made him wonder what she had thought of him all those years at the law firm.

CHAPTER 7

IT HAD BEEN ALMOST a week since she had talked to Max. What she'd said had bothered her, but he had called her adorable, and it had made her toes curl with excitement. Her toes didn't need to curl for Max Valentine.

Della knew she should have just ignored what he'd said and sent him on his way. He was not interested in her; Max was just looking for a friend. Tall blonde women were in short supply in Birch Cove, especially on Maple street.

Della had mainly lashed out because his flirting had been working, and she was ready to give into him. *Sleep with Max Valentine? Yes please,* her body had yelled. Her mind had regained control, and she went about it wrong. She needed to apologize.

It wasn't that she hadn't seen him, just that she hadn't talked to him. She saw him almost every night from her office couch since she could see straight into his bedroom. Della knew she should get blinds, but she kept putting it off. To be fair, he wasn't one to close curtains either. She was simply taking advantage of the view.

When Max had first moved in, she'd watched him organize his desk. He hadn't been wearing a shirt, which made her remember the fan she'd used when the house was being painted. She still had his number programmed into her phone from years ago as well. In reality, she hadn't expected him to answer her text. He had, and he had come over the moment she asked.

Now every night, she sat on her couch working, watching TV, and staring at him sitting in his room. He didn't type much. He read a lot. One night she thought about hiring him to work for her. Then she'd have someone else to do all the paperwork her job entailed.

Shaking her head, she dismissed the idea. Her life was busy enough without him and his flirting in it. She didn't need him in her life, and he would be gone soon anyway.

A little while later, she knocked on the Neilsons' door, hoping Max would be working, but secretly wanting to talk to him again.

Sally opened it with her signature excitement. "Hi, Sally. Evie sent some treats for you two—er, three." She added Max to her count.

"Come in! We were just having tea." She pulled Della into the house and then yelled, "Delly is here! She brought treats."

Walking through the house, Della tried to steel herself to see Max. It didn't work. He was gorgeous, just sitting drinking tea with no shirt on, and his hair was a little messed up. He ran his fingers through it when he was supposed to be writing—she watched him do it a lot. It made her want to run her fingers through it too.

"Hi, Mae, Max," Della said, trying to sound unaffected by his bare chest and all its muscles. "Evie sent some treats for you guys. She sent along extra for Max."

Evie had drilled her about the Max, and Della had tried to sound as nonchalant as possible about him. She hadn't wanted to tell her sister that she'd known Max for years ... or that he looked great without a shirt on. Not that her sister would care about Max's looks since she only had eyes for her husband.

"Let's see what she sent," Mae said as she took one of the plates from Della's hand, then turned to Max. "You need a shirt now. We have company. You can run around naked with us, but not Delphinea."

Della put the other plate down on the table, wishing he *was* running around naked. "It's fine, Max. I have to get home anyway. I wasted too much time at the farm today."

Sally opened the plastic covering the plate and asked, "How are the babies? And their mommies?"

"Everyone's good, and the mothers enjoying every minute of it," Della replied with a smile. She didn't want to talk about the babies; she wasn't a baby person.

Sally turned to Max. "Delly's sisters both had babies in the last two months. Zoey got married in the mansion at Christmas."

"It's a beautiful place, so I can see why she would want to get married there," Max said. He was staring at Della.

Was something wrong with her hair or something? Was her zipper down, or were her buttons not buttoned? She had put on jean shorts and a blue tank top, knowing how hot it was going to be out on the farm. Evie usually put her to work when she ventured out there.

"I have to go. Bye, everyone." She turned and fled from his probing eyes.

Smooth Della. So smooth, she taunted herself as she entered her house. After dropping her keys on the hall table, she went upstairs to her home. When she'd moved in, only the upstairs was livable, so she'd made it her own. Now she mostly lived up here, sometimes using the big kitchen downstairs, but usually was up in the five rooms that made up her house.

It was an odd setup, and nobody came up here but her. Even when her sisters came to visit, they went to main kitchen and hung out down there. So far, she hadn't found a man to bring home, and looking around town, she knew that probably wouldn't change any time soon.

After taking a long shower, she put on her usual lounge pants and T-shirt and was just settling down with her never-ending paperwork in her upstairs office when the doorbell rang. Della sighed, and as she went back down the stairs, she wondered who it could be. Maybe a neighbor kid? If it were family, they would've called first. Distracted, she swung open the door without looking to see who it was first. Expecting a kid or a neighbor, Della was completely taken aback when Mike Kelley, one of her client's ex's, stood glaring at her in the doorway. She hadn't seen him for a week, not since court. The ruling had gone his way, so why did he seem so angry with her?

Wide-eyed, she backed into the house, and he followed, yelling the entire time. "You little bitch! You think you can get away with this? Take my family from me? You have no right!"

Della stiffened her back as she reached for her phone in her pocket. She didn't have it. *Shit.* Taking a deep breath, she said, "I didn't do anything but help them. You're the one who made your family leave. Maybe if you didn't drink and hit the people you love, they wouldn't have had to—"

Before the last word left her mouth, his giant hand punched her full-on in the face. She hit the ground hard and felt him kick her in the stomach, then in the back when she curled into a ball to protect her organs. He'd stopped after the third kick, but she lay in a ball on the floor prepared for the next one. Her eyes were squeezed shut against the pain.

CHAPTER 8

MAX HAD BEEN STARING out the window when the large man stalked up Della's steps, shaking his head. He had instantly known something wasn't right. He raced down the stairs and was out the door before he had time to think about what he was doing. Della needed him.

As he left his aunts' house, he'd heard the yelling and had instantly called 911 on his phone. Before he made it to the middle of the street, the dispatch had summoned help. He hadn't known the address, but he'd said Della's name, and the dispatcher had known exactly who she was. Max had watched the man punch her in the face from the sidewalk.

Della was on the ground in a ball by the time he's made it up her steps. He threw himself at the giant man kicking at her. It hadn't moved the man much, but it had gotten his attention off her. Max knew he was this guy's newest victim and was ready for the blow when he heard sirens screaming down the road. Thank god this was a small town.

At the sound, the man whirled around and ran out the door. Max crawled over to Della who was still in a ball on the floor. Terror shot up his spine when she didn't move. "Della? Are you okay? Della!"

"No," she whispered.

He ran his hands over her body to see if anything was broken, relieved when he felt nothing unusual.

"Della, talk to me. Do you think anything's broken?" he asked, checking again.

"No? Maybe." she said.

Just then, a tall cop ran into the room and slid to a stop next to them. Max looked up and saw the concern in his eyes. He started checking her for wounds as he said, "An ambulance is coming. We got Kelley, and he should go to jail for this."

"No, no ambulance," she said, her eyes had cracked opened at the cop's voice.

"Della, why didn't you call the cops when you saw him?" the cop asked. Max realized he was the man who was with her at the farmer's market.

"I forgot my phone upstairs." She admitted, wincing as she tried to sit up.

"You're an idiot; a brilliant idiot. You know the house is wired, you just have to say one word, and it'll ring the station. You know a lot of men in this town aren't happy with you," the cop replied.

"I forgot. It happened pretty fast, Gabe." She had her head between her knees, breathing steadily.

Max sat back, still wanting to gather her into his arms and tell the cop to get out. The man seemed to share his level of concern for Della, except he didn't pull her into his arms either.

"Who's he?" Gabe gestured at Max.

"He's Max. He must have called the cops," Della said.

Max held out his hand. "Max Valentine. I'm staying with the sisters across the street."

Gabe grabbed his hand in a very firm handshake; too firm. "Gabe Watson. I'm married to her sister. Zoey's supposed to be the loose cannon, Della, not you."

"Sorry, sometimes the other cannon just goes off," Della replied with a weak laugh.

Gabe laughed at her joke and stood up, grabbing Della by the hand and pulling her to her feet. "If you can stand for five minutes, I will call off the ambulance." He looked at his watch. "Starting now."

"I can do it." Della swayed a little but stayed standing.

"You are pressing charges?" Gabe asked.

"Yes," Della said, shutting her eyes.

"Looks like he got you in the cheek, so you might have a black eye. It might turn some colors, but it shouldn't be too bad. Ribs?" Gabe just stared at his watch.

"I'll be sore, but nothing's broken."

Max stood up and asked, "Has this happened before?"

Gabe looked up from his watch, "She's not liked by some guys in the town, those who don't feel their wives should leave them. We patrol a lot, but sometimes they get by us."

Concerned, Max turned to the wobbly woman with her eyes closed. "You leave your door unlocked at lot, Della."

Gabe hissed at his sister-in-law. "Not what I want to hear, Connor Hart."

Della cracked one eye open and mumbled, "Don't listen then."

"Okay, that's five. No ambulance, but I *am* calling your sister the minute I'm out the door. She'll call Evie, and they'll both be calling or coming in. Get ready." Gabe walked out the door, closing it behind him.

Della slipped to the floor, then back in a ball. Max kneeled down beside her again. This time he ran his hand over her hair, over and over again. "Are you sure you don't want to see a doctor?"

Della's small voice came out of the ball. "Yes. No doctors."

He watched as she sat up and then stood wobbly on her legs again. Getting to his feet as well, he saw her look up the grand staircase. "Can I help you upstairs?"

Her green eyes turned to him. "Please."

Smiling at her, he easily lifted her into his arms and carried to her room. At the top, he looked around and saw five doors lining the hall. Three were closed, and two were open. The one in front of him had the biggest bed he had ever seen, a dark mahogany four-poster covered in a navy-blue comforter and sheets. He started towards it.

Della leaned her head on his shoulder and said, "Not the bedroom. Down at the end, the office."

So, he headed down to the other open door. "I don't think you can work, Della."

The words were spoken a little too soon because when he walked into the office, it was more like a living room, a living room whose walls were covered with built-in bookshelves. An overstuffed couch covered in pillows sat in a corner, and a large screen TV hung on a wall nearby. He carried her over to the couch and gently set her down.

Max grabbed a blanket and arranged it around her, then sat on the other end of the couch.

"You don't have to stay. I'm okay." She laid her head back against the couch.

He ignored her. "Do you need ice or anything?"

"No, I still have my water here from before." Della pointed at it.

"Does your head hurt?" he asked.

"My ribs hurt more, but I'm getting used to it."

"Pain killers?"

Della nodded. "Okay, go through the bedroom into the bathroom. They're in the cabinet above the sink."

He got up and walked back down the hallway to the bedroom. Walking past the giant bed, he noticed a large fireplace on the bedroom's far wall. Soon, he'd grabbed the bottle of pills and had turned to leave the room, coming face to face with the bed once more. He couldn't help but see her laying in that bed, red hair fanned out on the pillow.

Shutting down the image right there, he headed back to what she called the office. Della was sitting in the same spot and now talking on the phone. He sat down again and took out two pills and handed them to her, then handed her the glass of water. She smiled as she sat up and took the pills, then leaned back again.

Setting the water down, he grabbed a throw pillow and laid it on his lap. Then he slowly guided her head to rest on the pillow. Her feet settled on the other end of the couch, and he moved the blanket so that she was covered again.

"I'm fine," she said again into the phone. She had been facing away from him when he laid her down, but she'd rolled so she was facing straight up at the ceiling. He just watched her as she talked with her eyes closed.

"No, Zoey, you can't go punch him back. Gabe would be very mad at me for letting you," she replied, and he didn't hear what Zoey said. "I know you can knock him out for me."

He watched her shut her eyes tighter. He was worried for a minute, then her face relaxed again. "Yeah, I'm here. I'm going to put you on speaker, hold on." Opening her eyes, she looked at the phone and handed it to him. Taking it, he hit the button and held the phone so that the speaker was close to her mouth. But that meant the back of his hand was resting near her breasts.

"I'm back."

The voice out of the speaker was so close to Della's in tone he could tell they were sisters. "I can do something else if you want me to. I could take out the wiring in his truck. I've done it before. It takes forever to get it fixed."

Della rolled her eyes. "When? When did you do that, Zoey?"

"Junior prom, but I would do it again for you."

"No, Zoey, no retaliation. He's going to jail tonight anyway, and Gabe's working tonight. I hate to see him arrest you. Especially after he let you skate last year." Della gave a half grin half grimace at her statement.

"Let me skate?! He had no ground to stand on!" Zoey yelled through the phone.

"Don't be loud; it hurts my head. Fighting in a bar is a crime, punching a cop is a crime, and trying to get in said cop's pants within an hour *should* be a crime." Max could tell Della was enjoying teasing her sister by the smile on her face.

"I have a good lawyer," Zoey argued. "And I wasn't trying to get in his pants. I was just going to kiss the shit out of him."

"Also a little illegal, Zoey. He was on duty." Della opened her green eyes.

Looking down at her, he lifted an eyebrow in question. She smiled nodded at him, then winced and put her hand to her head. He was enjoying just being with her.

"You need to marry a cop," Zoey said from the phone.

"I don't need to marry anyone, Zoey."

"But if you marry a cop, he can protect you, and you can fight crime together. He can catch them, and you can lock them up." Zoey was serious.

Della broke out in a fit of laughter and held her head. The cartoon that had formed in his mind had him smothering a chuckle himself.

"No cops. I'll have to fight crime by myself." Della's voice was still filled with laughter.

"Officer Rick's available. He's nice," Zoey stated, testing the water.

"Too old. He's older than Gabe," Della pointed out. Max wondered how old Gabe was.

"Officer Dan's very nice," Zoey said with a purr.

"I think I'll have to tell Gabe about your fascination with officer Dan, who is—don't make me do math—younger than me by a lot." Della looked up at Max and winked.

Zoey sighed in exasperation. "Only just over ten years, and I think he's man enough for you."

Max watched Della's face turn pink in his lap. "He can barely drink legally, Zoey Hart."

"How about—" Zoey started.

"Stop, no more," Della talked over her sister. Both sisters were silent for a bit.

"Gabe said there was a guy at your place with no shirt on. Who was it? Tell me everything." Zoey asked over the phone. Della could tell Zoey was grinning.

Her eyes flew to his and she blushed again, deeper this time. "He's Mae's grandnephew, and he's staying with her and Sally to write a book."

"In the house?" Zoey asked.

"Yes, he's in the turret room. I think he saw Mike show up and knew something was wrong because he came over and called the cops. I'm lucky he did too. I don't know what the jerk would've done if no one had showed up." Then she mouthed thank you to him.

He started to run his hand over the spot she had touched when she'd winced. Her hair was softer than he had expected, and the curls liked to bounce back.

"Does he know if they share a room?" Zoey asked. She was very interested in his great aunts.

"You'll have to ask him if you meet him, or I can ask him for you if you want," Della said and smiled up at him.

"Oh, I'll meet him." The confidence in Zoey's voice was palpable.

Della's phone in his hand buzzed with another call. It said "E."

"Evie's calling, I have to go," Della told her sister.

"Tell her to call me when you get done."

"So, you two can talk about me?" Della asked.

"Yes, we have to compare notes."

"I will. Bye, Zoey. Love you."

"Love you too, Della."

When Zoey hug up the phone, the office was quiet. "Thank you for helping me. I'm feeling better, but I have another call coming."

"You and your sisters are really close," Max commented. "Do I want to meet Zoey?"

She smiled at him and said, "Oh, yes. Your life will be changed when you meet her. She'll have lots of questions about how you saved me, and of course, questions about Mae and Sally."

"You were right about seeing that man and knowing something wasn't right. I just wished I'd moved faster. And I don't know if I have the answers about my aunts. They're eccentric."

"If that's what you kids are calling it these days." Della shrugged as the phone rang again.

Max answered it for her, so she wouldn't have to lift her head, and he placed it on speaker immediately. He was rewarded with a smile from Della.

He grinned back as she said, "Evie, I'm fine, and you're on speaker phone."

"You know I don't like speaker phone," came the voice, another copy of Della's.

"Sorry, my head hurts too much to hold the phone."

"I'm going to come in and take care of you. No, wait, I'll come and get you and bring you back here. Get you out of that house." Evie sounded as if she were gathering her things to do just that.

"No, we'll both stay put. I'm fine, and I've taken something for the pain. I'll sleep it off and be right as rain tomorrow," Della said matter-of-factly.

"Are you tired? Do you have a concussion?"

Della rolled her eyes. "I have a sister who made me pick strawberries for two hours today and then made me help her make jelly for another five. I'm beat."

"So, no concussion?" Evie asked again.

"No."

"Black eyes?"

"No."

"Broken bones?"

"No."

"Are there going to be more patrols past your house for a while?"

"Yes, I think Gabe will make sure of it." Della assured her.

"I'm going to send you some stuff tomorrow. Jasper will drop it off when he goes to work," Evie said as if some stuff would make all the difference in her recovery.

"What stuff?" Della's eyes were on the ceiling again.

Evie hedged. "Just some stuff for you to eat. I know you don't eat when you're sick. And … some other stuff."

"Take the extra stuff out of the box; just the food please. And have him leave it on the porch since I might sleep in tomorrow. I deserve it, I think," Della replied while staring at the ceiling.

"Okay, I'll tell Jasper."

"Thank you, Evie." Della yawned.

"Are you sure you're okay?" Evie asked with deep concern.

"Yes, I'll be fine. I'm just going to bed after I'm done talking to you," Della said.

"I'll call you during the night, and if you don't answer, I am coming in," Evie warned.

Della sighed. "Don't call please."

"You can't stop me."

"Fine, but not too often. Just because you have a baby to wake you up every hour doesn't mean you can call me every time you're up. Once, before 3:00 a.m. *Once*," Della argued.

"Fine, but you'll say something when I do call you."

"Fine. Call Zoey for me. She doesn't get to call me also."

"Fine. I love you. Goodbye," Evie said.

"Love you too."

Max ended the call and placed the phone on the coffee table. Della's eyes were closed, and she looked exhausted. He had been running his hand over her hair for most of the second call but stopped when she'd hung up. Not knowing what to do with his other hand, he placed it on her stomach above the blanket.

"Thanks again," she said.

"Are you sure you're okay? I saw some of those kicks; he wasn't holding back." Max's frowned, remembering the vicious kicks. They were going to be in his mind for a long time.

"It wasn't as bad as it looked. He got in a few good blows, but I was ready for it." Della was looking at the ceiling again.

"You were ready for it?" he questioned.

"Yeah. Zoey taught me how to take a punch—and a kick, for that matter." Della smiled at him.

"Zoey, the one who said she'd battle this guy for you?" he asked, returning her grin.

"Yep. Last year she took on four brothers at once. She had two of them down before Gabe hauled her out of the bar." There was pride in her voice.

Max raised an eyebrow at her. "When did your sister teach you these tricks?"

"About a month after I opened my doors and another husband pounded me into the ground. That time I was in the hospital overnight."

"So, this happens a lot?"

"No, just every once in a while. When they've spent years beating their wives, it's no stretch to start taking it out on me," Della said, eyes shut again.

"Where did your sister learn all of this?"

She explained. "Army. She was in for eight years. Gabe was a marine for twenty, and I think they teach each other moves. I don't really ask about it."

"So, your sister must be taller than you to get into the military," he said with a chuckle.

Della narrowed her eyes at him. "Low, Valentine. I wouldn't be so short if you weren't so tall. And Zoey is as short as me. Shorter even."

"Is that why you wear all those tall heels? To be taller? I saw today, and you wore just tennis shoes like a normal woman." He had been completely surprised when she'd delivered the treats to the sisters. Except when she was barefoot, he hadn't seen her in anything shorter than three-inch heels.

"I wear heels because I enjoy wearing heels," she stated firmly.

He watched her eyes close again; exhaustion was setting in. He kept stroking the red curls on her head. It seemed to relax her, so he kept doing it. It didn't hurt that he was enjoying being able to touch her.

"Do you want to go to bed?" he asked.

Della smiled, not opening her eyes. "Nice. Coming on to a hurt woman."

"I didn't mean it like that," he stated.

"I know, I was just making fun of the playboy." She sat up and scooted to the edge of the couch. If she was in pain, she didn't show it.

Standing up, he took her into his arms again. This time he didn't ask where to take her, his mind had made an easy-to-follow map to her bedroom. When he got there, he pulled back the covers with one hand and gently placed her into the bed. Della immediately slid across the bed to the other side.

His face must have shown some reaction because she said, "This is my side." Then she placed her phone on the nightstand. "Thank you again for doing all this for me. I know you had better things to do."

"There's nothing I would rather have been doing than making sure you are okay," he answered softly as she laid her head on the pillow, then rolled away from him. His image of her hair on the pillow was a pale comparison to the real thing.

Max's mind yelled at him as he turned away. After a snap decision, he changed his mind and kicked off his shoes. Turning back to the bed, he climbed in beside her. He knew Della wanted someone there with her, even if she was going to be stubborn about it. He gathered her into his arms so that her back was pressed to his chest, and he was a little surprised she didn't pull away.

Max brought the covers up around them and realized that he still wasn't wearing a shirt; he had gotten chilly. The combination of her body and the blankets was amazing. Add in the smell of her hair, and the feeling was familiar and exotic at the same time.

It took only a few minutes for her breathing to settle into a steady pattern. Della had fallen asleep. He glanced at the clock on her side of the bed. It wasn't even 6:00 p.m. yet. The last two hours had been draining. Beside the clock he saw a picture of three women on the grand staircase. The bride looked so much like Della, as did her other sister. Their faces were nearly identical, but it was the two redheads that had captivated him. They were so alike, and as he looked, he realized the bride was adorable, but his Della was gorgeous.

Laying back, he pulled that gorgeous woman a little closer to him. She made a noise in the back of her throat as she settled against his chest. Slowly, he placed his hand on her delicate stomach to keep himself from straying north or south.

Max smiled and closed his eyes, enjoying just having her in his arms. Who knew if he'd get this chance with her again, so he wasn't going to mess it up.

CHAPTER 9

DELLA WOKE from the most erotic dream she had ever had. Max Valentine was the star, and she wanted to go back. Her body was turned on, and she wanted to finish. She arched her back, pushing her breasts further into his hand. It tightened around her in response, and she moaned at the sensation.

The hand was real. Her eyes flew open, and she wondered for a moment who's hand it was. The events of the previous evening flashed through her mind as she realized it had to be Max. Max, who had saved her from Mike Kelley. Max, who had taken care of her. Max, who was in bed with her.

He had been so nice to her, taking care of her even after she had told him not to. If it hadn't been for Max, she would still be on the floor downstairs. She never would have made it up all those steps on her own.

Slowly she rolled out of his arms, careful not to wake him. It was just past midnight, and he was sleeping so peacefully. Damn him for being gorgeous when he slept, especially in her bed. How was she supposed to get that image out of her head?

Grabbing her phone, she left him and went down the hall to her upstairs office. As she walked, her side was sore, but her cheek was okay. It might be bruised, but it didn't hurt, and it wasn't swollen.

Della left the office door open a crack and turned the light on. The room looked like it always did, but something was missing tonight. *Max with no shirt, sitting on her couch—that's what's missing*, she thought to herself.

Sitting on the couch, she gathered the blanket around her and looked out her windows at the Neilsons' house across the street. Max's light was still on, and she could see into his empty room. Maybe she should invest in curtains or blinds if Max was going to stay too long. She hated to lose the light and airiness the large windows provided. But how was she going to tell Max that he should close his curtains if he didn't want her to see him. That she might be watching, *was watching*.

Della pulled the blanket closer and wondered if she should go back to bed with Max. *No, let him sleep*, she told herself. She wouldn't be sleeping anymore; she'd gotten in close to six hours. That was an hour more than usual for her, and Evie would be calling soon. The phone would wake up Max.

She pulled her laptop off the coffee table and turned it on. Might as well get some work done. While the computer booted up, she pulled out her phone and sent a text to both of her sisters.

Della: Not dead, fine.

When the computer was on, she pulled a legal pad to her and starting on a brief she needed to get done by the end of the day.

Zoey: How are the bruises?

Della had known her sisters would be up at some point, both had tiny babies in the house. Nights were no longer for sleeping. Zoey was not a big sleeper anyway, Della had learned that after Zoey had left the army. Neither sister needed more than 4 hours to function. That had made college easier, she could study more than other students.

Della: Good. Just a little sore.

In the last six months Della, had written so many of these briefs she could usually get them done in an hour. This one was no different. Her fingers flew across the keypad without her even thinking about what she was writing.

Zoey: Gabe said the neighbor boy had no shirt on.

Della picked up the phone and smiled. He looked so good with no shirt on. Probably looked good in her bed with no shirt on. Maybe she should go back and look.

Della: He's living at Mae's house, no AC.
Zoey: He doesn't know about them at all?
Della: He calls them sisters all the time.
Zoey: I love this.
Della: I'll have to tell him. I just wanted to see how long it took to notice.

Zoey didn't respond back. That's what happens when you have a baby: duty calls. Della went back to her brief. She had sent it to the printer downstairs when Evie finally called.

"Are you sure you're okay?"

"Yes, just a little sore. I should be fine by morning. Zoey's tricks worked this time," Della said with a smile. Evie hadn't been excited when Zoey showed her the self-defense moves.

"Yeah, this time, but what about next time? How are you going to be after that one? Are you going to be in the hospital then?" Evie asked. She hated when her sister worried about her. She had spent her adult life not letting Evie worry about her. Della was the older sister, so she was the one who was supposed to be worried.

Della knew ways to get Evie off her back. "Are you breastfeeding that baby while you yell at me?"

"Yes, and her name is Willow, not 'that baby.'" Evie was quieter than before.

"I know her name, Evie. Willow Hart Reed. See? I know the whole thing."

"Are you going to be her godmother?" Evie asked, not for the first time.

"Have Zoey be it. It will be cuter if Zoey and Gabe are Willow's godparents, and you and Jasper are Connor's. See, I know his name to." Della wasn't going to be a godparent this time around. She was already Ben's, Evie's twelve-year-old son. The family had changed a lot since those years. The two couples could take over the little rituals without dragging her into it.

"If that's what you want," Evie said quietly, Della knew she had hurt her sister's feelings.

"I just can't, Evie. It's been too much lately out there," Della replied, meaning the farm and the babies and the couples in love.

"Are you ever going to hold one of them?" Evie asked.

Della looked at the phone. She hadn't thought anyone had noticed she hadn't held either her niece or nephew since they were born. At first, she claimed they were too small, then she had always managed to find something else to do. Each baby had two devoted parents to hold them. She didn't know how long it would last until they noticed. Apparently, not long enough.

Della took a breath and felt the tears threatening her eyes as she said, "I don't know, Evie. I don't think I can."

"Della, you have to talk about this. Maybe not with me, but with someone."

A tear slipped out of Della's eye and ran down her cheek as she answered her sister, "Talking won't change what happened, Evie. I have to go."

Della hung up on her sister. She didn't want to talk about it, and Evie wasn't going to make her. It had been months since she had told her sister her secret. They had barely acknowledged what had been said the day Evie was helping her paint her bedroom ... the bedroom Max was sleeping in.

Evie had spent weeks moping around because the man she loved had moved back to Minneapolis.

Della had blown up at her younger sister, who thought that her life was so messed up and that nothing in her life had ever gone her way. Della had just moved home and into Evie's house while the mansion was getting ready. She had watched Evie get depressed about everything from Jasper being younger than her, to her having had a bad first marriage and having raised her son on her own. Della couldn't keep her mouth shut anymore, and she'd told her she was lucky to have a man who loved her, even if she wasn't even trying to make it work. She was lucky to have a job she loved and that she was doing what she wanted to do. Della had been fired a few weeks before from the job she had thought that she loved.

But then Della had let her mouth get away from her and told her sister that she should never complain about raising her son because at least she got to keep him. Della's own child had been put up for adoption. Evie had never known about that, and Della wished she still didn't know. She didn't want anyone to know.

The computer screen blurred from the tears filling her eyes. She didn't let herself think about that time, ever, and now Evie had brought it up.

Evie had only been fourteen and had no idea what had been going on with her sister that year. Though the sisters were only two years apart in age, Della had been smart and driven and had graduated from high school three years early. By the time Della was fifteen, she was already at the university in Minneapolis. Taking high school classes when you were younger than your peers was easy. In Birch Cove, even if kids were older then you, you still know everyone.

University was completely different. She'd felt out of place and had a hard time settling in. A large load of classes filled her time, but she still had no one to eat or study with. Her dorm roommates loved to party, but Della hadn't. She had been completely alone.

Then one night, her three roommates insisted she join them at a party. It was Friday night, and her dad wasn't coming to pick her up for the weekend. It was harvest, and he couldn't make the four-hour round trip to get her. She was still too young to have gotten her driver's license.

Within an hour, she was happy she'd gone. After two beers, she was feeling pretty good, and then she saw him. Tall, dark, and handsome was the only way to describe the young man who'd come right up to her and said hi. Her head had spun from the fact that a boy was talking to her, and maybe because of the alcohol.

He'd offered her another glass of beer, and she drank it as they talked. To this day, she had no idea what they had talked about. His name had been lost to that night as well. Had he put something in her drink, or had she just drunk too much? She never knew. When she'd woken up, her roommates were gone, and she'd been naked and alone in a strange bedroom. Della had pulled on her clothes as fast as she could and quietly walked through the house that the party had been in. It was a mess, and everybody had left. It had been a long walk back to campus, but she needed the time to figure out what had happened.

Eighteen years later, she still didn't know what happened. As she'd made her way back to her dorm, she knew they'd had had sex because she was in so much pain. When she got to the room, her roommates didn't say anything to her, and she didn't say anything to them. Within a month, she had gotten reassigned to her own room. She couldn't deal with people and didn't want to learn how.

By Christmas vacation, she knew she was pregnant, and all the wishing in the world wouldn't make it go away. At the end of her vacation, she'd told her dad. She hadn't know how he was going to take the news, but anger was the way he'd responded. He'd yelled at her, saying that she was the smart one and that she knew better. He had a thirteen-year-old and a nine-year-old at home, and his wife had left him three years before. He couldn't deal with a fifteen-year-old being pregnant.

Looking back, she wondered if he really saw her as a fifteen-year-old. Since her mother had taken off in the night, leaving him to raise three girls on his own, Charley Hart had leaned on Della. She had taken responsibility for the younger girls, getting them ready for school and helping them with their homework in the evenings. Most of the time, she had to feed them since he'd been busy working on the farm. But over the years, Della had watched Evie farm and raise a son on her own, and she did it without much complaining or help from anyone.

After Christmas break that year, instead of going home again, Della had stayed in school and studied. She'd taken another heavy load the next semester to keep her mind occupied, and luckily, she'd actually had an easy pregnancy and had not been sick once. No one in the dorms or in her classes even suspected anything. She'd just started to wear sweatpants and sweatshirts all the time, like most college kids.

When the spring semester had ended, she'd stayed on campus for summer classes. She hadn't seen her father in nearly six months when he showed up on campus to see her. He'd taken her out for lunch and informed her she would put the baby up for adoption, deciding she was too young to deal with these things. And if she had kept it, he would no longer support her, and he wouldn't let her see her sisters. He was making arrangements with a company that handled these things.

"These things," he had said, not "her baby," and not "his grandchild," just "these things." Had she wanted to keep the baby? Yes, she wanted it. It was hers no matter what. She loved the little baby growing in her belly, but she'd had no way to support it when it was born. At the time, she wasn't even sixteen, and even though she had a year of college under her belt, she would have a hard time getting a job.

That baby had been born on Friday, July 25, at 7:00 p.m. Della knew that date well—she had turned sixteen that day. She had called her dad when the labor had started, but he'd said Evie had a softball game, and he wanted to see it. Della had given birth to her baby girl alone.

The nurse had handed her the baby, and Della soaked in her daughter, who had beautiful dark hair. Her eyes were blue, like all babies', and Della had wondered what color they would be later. The baby had cried in her arms and wiggled to get closer to Della like she, too, knew this was their only time together. Hugging the tiny baby to her, she swore it was better for her daughter to live with another family. Della wasn't good for the baby.

Lightly touching her baby's fine black hair, she'd named the baby Natalie, knowing the new family would name her something else. But to Della, she would be her Natalie. She was stared at the baby she would never see again until she'd passed out.

When she'd came to, her Natalie was gone. The doctor had came in and said there had been some complications. Della had started to hemorrhage while holding the baby, and they had rushed her to surgery. They had ended up doing a complete hysterectomy right there; the baby had been big, and Della was not.

Saturday morning, her dad had finally come to the hospital. If he had seen her baby, she never knew. Della never saw her again. That morning a woman came in with the paperwork for her to sign. That was the only time she saw her daughter's birth certificate. Natalie Hart was the name on the government document. Della had signed everywhere she was told to, crying the entire time. When the lady finally left to take her daughter from her forever, her father just looked at her and said, "That's done."

She stayed in the hospital for another four days. Her father never came back. Nobody came to visit. There were no flowers or cards in her room, just her and her misery. The day she was released, she'd stuffed everything about that week down and never talked about it to anyone.

Except once, with her father when, six years later, Evie ended up pregnant during her freshman year of college. In May, she gave birth to a baby boy and brought it home to the house their father had bought for her and her husband. Della had come home from Minneapolis, where she was just starting her new job as a lawyer to see the new baby. After the first visit her dad had walked her out to the car as she was leaving and said, "You would rather have a great job than a baby."

Turning before she got into the car, she replied, "No, I would rather have my baby back." After getting in, she slammed the door and never looked at him again. He died seven years later, and they'd never talked about it again. In fact, they had never gotten to a good place in their relationship before he died. Evie had an amazing relationship with their father, and Della wished she'd had that same relationship, but there was no coming back from what had happened that week in July.

Della had never tried to find Natalie, knowing she had a family and life of her own. She didn't need Della. For years, Della had known she could send a letter to the adoption agency that handled her case, and they would've forwarded the letter to her baby, but Della had never done it. The pain would be too great if she didn't get a letter back.

Della blew her nose and put the laptop on the coffee table again. Taking out another tissue, she wiped her face, then quietly retraced her steps to her bedroom. Max was still sleeping, now on his back. His chest wasn't covered by blankets, and it was glorious.

Rubbing her face with her hands, she walked quietly through the room her room and into the adjoining bathroom. She closed the pocket door behind her and then turned on the light.

She needed a shower more than anything to wash the memories off her. She stripped down and climbed into the shower as it beat down ice cold water onto her skin, letting the cold wash away the pain as warm water started to come through the pipes.

With all the babies around here now, no wonder her memories were resurfacing. It was only two months until her daughter's eighteenth birthday, and Della's thirty-fourth. It was always the hardest day, and this time, she was living in the same town as her sisters. She didn't want to spend the day with them, but so far, she had no way of getting out of it.

The water was turning cold again when she shut it off. She was feeling so much better; even her sides weren't as painful as they had been. Drying off, she wondered if Max would cooperate if she climbed back into bed and seduced him. She could use a warm body tonight.

Over the years, she had managed to date men, but her work hours had made it nearly impossible, and when they'd stopped calling, she'd barely noticed. After a few dates and a few rolls in the hay, she was ready to move on. As much as she'd teased Max about being a play-boy, she was really no better.

She shut off the light in the bathroom before slowly opening the door. Quietly, she walked through the room. When she was half-way across, he sat up, and she gasped. "You scared me!"

"Are you okay?" he asked sleepily. He was sitting up, and the blanket had pooled around his waist.

"I'm fine. Go back to bed."

"Why aren't you in bed?" he asked.

"I slept, then I woke up and Evie called," she said, knowing it really didn't sound right. Maybe he was too tired to notice.

"Are you okay?" he asked again.

She forced a laugh. "Yes, now go back to bed." She left the room and headed down the hall to her upstairs office again.

Sitting down on her couch, she pulled her computer on her lap and started it up. She was trying to figure out where she was on the document when Max sat down next to her.

"You don't have to stay," she said.

"You shouldn't be working," he countered.

"Why? I'm fine."

He looked at her, concerned. "Don't you have a headache?"

"No, I'm fine really. I have three briefs due tomorrow, and I need to get these last two done."

"Don't you have tomorrow to do them then?"

She looked up at him and saw he was sitting in his shorts. He still didn't have a shirt on, and he looked cold. "Are you cold?"

"No," he said.

Della gave him a flat look. "Liar." She put the computer to her side and pulled off her blanket, then flipped it over him.

"Thanks, but I was fine." He snuggled into the warm blanket.

"I'm trying to be nicer to you," she replied as she shut her computer again and turned to him. "I am sorry about last week. What I said was just mean; I know it. I know you aren't interested in me, and I shouldn't have said the thing about the air conditioning."

"Okay," he said.

She had no idea how to take that, but she was happy she hadn't jumped him a few minutes ago. It would have ended badly.

"Are you hungry? Did you eat before you came over?" she asked when she realized she hadn't eaten in over twelve hours.

"No. Actually, yes. I could eat." Max nodded.

"Come on, then. We can find you a shirt downstairs too."

Not waiting to see if he was following, she headed out of the room and down the hall. Food would settle her roller coaster of emotions. At the top of the stairs, he grabbed her around the waist. Della almost leaned into his strong arms but caught herself.

Max raised an eyebrow at her. "Are you sure you can do the stairs?"

She turned on the lights that illuminated the stairway. "Yep."

He followed her as she walked down the stairs; she could feel his presence behind her. "Your hair is a lot curlier when it's wet."

Reaching up, she touched the red locks. She knew that they looked like Shirley temple ringlets in red. She hadn't even tried to brush them out after her shower. "I know, I've been fighting it my whole life."

When she got to the bottom of the stairs, she turned away from the office area and headed into the ballroom. Yes, her house had its own gorgeous ballroom. Flipping on the lights, she walked to the closet where Chad kept his stuff. He didn't keep much here, but he did keep a change of clothes in case he got to dirty while working.

She pulled a shirt from the top, making a mental note to wash and replace it tomorrow. Della moved to hand the shirt over and saw Max standing in the middle of the room, turning in a slow circle and looking at the room around him. She smiled at the image of a shirtless Max staring at the gorgeous room. "It's the ballroom. I haven't figured out what to do with it yet. We had Zoey's wedding reception in here."

She handed him the shirt, and he slipped it on as he said, "It's amazing. This whole house is amazing."

"Thank you. I love it here. I never thought I could be happy back in Birch Cove, but this house makes me happy every day." She took his hand and pulled him back out to the kitchen.

She shut the light off as they left and went past the stairway and through her office area and into the kitchen. This was the most boring room in the house, and it desperately needed an update. By the looks of it, the kitchen had last been updated in the sixties. Once winter set in, she would have him focus on it.

"You didn't want to come back here?" he asked, taking a seat on a stool as she looked into the fridge.

As Della pulled out the makings for sandwiches, she couldn't believe he asked that. "Max, I was fired, and I had no place else to go. I came home with my tail between my legs."

"You seem to like it here." He shrugged.

"I had lived away from here for longer than I'd lived here. I loved corporate law, and I was so close to partner. I would've made partner before I was thirty-five, and then everything was gone. I could never work in that town again."

Max was cutting cheese. "But you enjoy it here. I never saw you smile at the office. You're a completely different person now."

When she looked up, he was watching her. "I haven't changed anything but my hair, Max. When I started, I had a hard time meeting new people, but by the time I was ready to be friends with you guys, the moment was gone. I was just Dee, and nobody paid attention to me or invited me places. I was never actually invited on your retreats."

Max handed her the sliced cheese, and she placed it on the sandwiches, then slid the plates onto the island next to them.

"I did notice you. We started the same day, and you had the office next to mine for years. You knew case law, and if anyone had a question, you usually knew the answer or found it within hours," Max said.

She went and grabbed two cans of soda from the fridge and a bag of chips from beside it. She should let it go, but she needed him to hear it. "You didn't know my name for nearly a year after we met."

"I knew it, but it was weird, and it took me a while to say it. DC … it doesn't roll off the tongue. You never called me Max, always Valentine. So, I started to call you Hart, but then that sounded … I don't know." He frowned, looking away.

"Like an endearment?"

"Yeah, like I was calling you honey or something."

"That's why I changed it. I added the Connor because it felt like that a lot. My sister Zoey did it too. I didn't get married, ever," she said, sitting next to him.

"Connor was your mom's maiden name? Hence the Connor Mansion, I assume."

Della nodded. "Yeah, my mom grew up here, but I never think of her here. I haven't seen her since I was twelve, so I don't remember much about her. I do get to see her every day in the mirror, but I know very little about her," Della admitted.

"So, you changed your name to Delphinea Connor Hart. What was it when you were born?" He changed the subject, and she was grateful.

"Delphinea Connor Hart," she stated simply.

"I know that, but what was it at birth?"

"Do I need to pull out my birth certificate? I just shifted my middle name to my first last name. I don't have a middle name now. My mother named all her daughters with Connor as the middle name. It was a legacy." Della rolled her eyes.

"No wonder you never really noticed it then. Your name really didn't change."

"So how much younger are your sisters then you?" he asked,

"Two and six years. Evie is two, and Zoey's the baby. They farm together. Both are married now and, of course, have a baby each. Evie has Ben also, who's twelve now. How about you? Any siblings?"

"I also have two sisters. Hannah is my full sister at one year older than me—she lords it over me too. She's married to John, the job you wouldn't take, John, and they have two little kids. Sarah is twenty-three, and we share a mother. You met Sarah at the farmer's market," he replied slyly.

She hissed. "Sarah was your sister? Why did you let me say all those things about her?"

"Because I thought it was cute you were jealous." He grinned.

"I was *not* jealous," she said, knowing she was lying to him.

"Liar." He laughed. "Why don't you wear glasses anymore?"

Taking a drink of her pop, she raised her eyebrows at him. Then she put the can down and said, "Glasses? I don't know what you are talking about."

"You're going with that answer, Hart?"

"I have perfect vision."

"Tell me," he demanded with a smile.

Della gave in and sighed. "They made me look older. I'm cursed with a baby face."

Max suppressed a laugh. "You seriously wore them for ten years just to make yourself look older?"

"They made me feel older too, okay. How old to I look? Truth." she asked, looking into his gray eyes.

He looked back and smiled. "Right now, with your crazy hair, I would card you before I served you a drink."

"See? Zoey gets carded all the time, and she's twenty-eight! Last week at the farmers market, a woman asked her if she'd graduated this year." It had been that way for years. "Last year, when I took her to Vegas for her birthday, and we got tattoos, he wouldn't do anything until he saw our IDs to make sure we were old enough to consent. You don't want to know how many times I took out that ID for drinks."

"Wait, what?" He took her hand that had been flailing around during her rant. "First you have a tattoo that I'll talk to you about later. Second, your math isn't adding up. Your sister is twenty-seven?"

"Twenty-eight now."

"Twenty-eight, and you're six years older than her? So, thirty-four?"

"No, I'm thirty-three. I haven't had my birthday yet, so we're around six years apart." She explained.

"But you started at the law firm when I did. I started when I graduated, and so did you. I am thirty-seven, almost thirty-eight," he replied, still holding her hands.

How had she let the numbers out? She hated when people knew she had skipped grades. They always treated her different. Della bit her lip she they looked into his eyes and smiled. *Fine, let him look at her different.* "I skipped kindergarten and fifth grade. Then I had enough credits to graduate when I was a junior, and I made it through undergrad in three years instead of four."

He laughed. "Mae and Sally are always saying how brilliant you are. I thought it was because you were a lawyer, but it's because you're just brilliant. So how old were you when you started at the firm"

"Twenty-one. I turned twenty-two a few months later. I could do the job, but the people part was hard for me then." Her forehead creased a little at the memory.

"I can imagine. I was four years older than you and felt that the work was the hard part. The people were easy," he admitted.

"You had a hard time in the beginning too?" She had never thought of things being hard for Max Valentine; life seemed easy for him.

"Everyone did. It was never just you, Della," Max said.

"It always felt like it was just me." She watched him shake his head.

"What happened with Grant Miller?" he asked.

She hated that name, but suddenly, she wanted Max to know it all. "Grant asked me out, and I said yes. He was a nice guy, or so I'd thought. It was in the early spring, before I'd gotten fired. I didn't know he was married, and I really didn't have close friends at the firm, so nobody to gossip with. We went out three times. Every time he tried to get me to take him home with me, but I really wasn't ready for that with him, and I lived in Maple Grove." The suburb was twenty minutes from the downtown area.

She took a deep breath. "It lasted for almost four weeks. So, three dates in four weeks, but he would come into my office all the time and want to talk to me. I was flattered. I wish I hadn't been, but I was. After the first week, he'd started to take folders from my desk. Then he'd started to get my cases shifted to him, just as they were wrapping up. I was starting to notice he was doing it more and more. It didn't stop after I ended our relationship. That's when I found out he was married and to who. I was going to Milton on that Monday morning with what I knew, but Grant had talked to him over the weekend. The benefit of being married to the boss's daughter."

"Nobody was going to believe me. Grant was a stud, and I was nothing. I never even slept with him, and it still destroyed my career." She looked up from where their hands were connected on the counter to see his gray eyes boring into hers. He seemed to believe her.

"Grant's a prick. You're not the only one in the office he was stealing cases from. He hadn't done his own work in years! When I left, I told Milton that Grant would send his company into the ground in month if he took over. I also told him that you were the most knowl-edgeable lawyer in the building, and he had let you go."

"You said that about me?" she asked, eyebrows raising in surprise.

"Yes."

"Thank you, Max."

Move, she demanded her body. She was wanting to fall into his arms and stay there. So, she gathered the empty plates and took them to the sink.

"Why did you live in Maple Grove?"

"Cheap rent. I didn't want to waste my money on something downtown. I had other things to spend my money on," she said simply.

"What?"

Raising her arms out, she answered, "I had to pay for this baby."

"The mansion?"

"When my dad died, I created a trust for the properties the three of us inherited. It was quite a bit, and Evie was getting sacked with most of it. Two farms of significant size, and this place. So, I put everything in trust. It was all paid off, so we had no payments. Evie was twenty-five, had a little kid, and was going to start farming by herself. Zoey was in Afghanistan, and I was away in Minneapolis. The trust insured that Evie wasn't sacked at tax time, and the property wasn't broken up before we were ready to deal with it."

"I'm Impressed," Max said with a nod.

"So last year, when Zoey left the Army, she received the farm we grew up on. The house was empty, and Evie was using the yard for her gardens and chickens. Then I came home, and Evie said I had to fix this place up and move in. It was a great decision," she added.

"You got the best deal."

"You didn't see it last year. I've spent most of my savings on Chad and fixing up the place. Gabe paid for some of it to get it ready for the wedding, but it's taken so much money. I've had Chad here every day for over seven months. I really need a secretary, but I pay him instead. Filing will have to wait until he's done."

"How much longer do you think it will take?" he asked.

"It'll take most of the summer to paint. There are seven colors in this house. Seven," she said, holding up the appropriate number of fingers. "Then there's the kitchen."

He just laughed at her, and she laughed with him. It was good to have someone to talk to.

"How's your head?"

"Good. No pain, thanks for asking."

"Are you tired yet?"

"Are you?"

"I could sleep," he said with a smirk.

"I can't. I've had enough sleep for tonight. I don't usually sleep much," she admitted.

"I don't want to leave you alone yet. Do you want to watch a movie on that giant TV?" he asked.

"You're just jealous. I've seen Sally's TV." She grabbed a bag of candy bars from the cabinet.

"I am jealous. It's bigger than mine at home," he replied, turning to walk through her entire house to get to the TV room.

"Sorry to hear yours is so small, Valentine." She followed him up the stairs.

When she got to the top, she ducked into the bathroom. Quickly, she brushed the ringlets out of her hair, she hated those. Once she made it to the office, he was already on the couch. She had grabbed the blanket off the bed since her throw was too small for two people. Max was staring out the window as she sank into the couch beside him, right into the bedroom he slept in.

"Did you know you can see right into the turret room from here?" he questioned.

"Mhmm."

Max looked at her and grinned. "So, you watch me?"

"No, I see you sometimes, but I don't watch." She defended herself. "I'll get blinds tomorrow, and they'll be up by tomorrow night. Sorry, I should have done it a week ago." She had been so excited to spend more time with him, but instead that per usual, she was a fool.

He broke the tension. "I guess it's a good thing that I don't spend all evening naked then. Or is it a bad thing?"

She felt her cheeks burning at the thought of him naked, wandering around the room. "Do what you want. It's your room."

"Maybe I should start watching you in the evenings." He turned and looked at her again. "The ringlets are gone. You brushed them out."

Her hand went up to her hair, "I don't like the tight curls. And don't bother looking up here in the evenings, I'm just on my computer."

His eyebrow shot up. "Naked?"

"No!" She laughed. "Just like this, usually."

"Shoot. Maybe naked one day," he said and grabbed the remote from her coffee table.

She snatched it out of his hands with a wink. "My TV, my choice."

She turned on the TV, and he grabbed the blanket and arranged it around them.

Max pulled her close to him. She let it happen, allowing her body to relax into his. "Tell me if you see anything you're interested in." She flipped through the movies on the screen. He stopped her three movies in, and she started to play it. Putting the remote down, she picked up her legal pad and a pen.

He softly laughed and grabbed it out of her hand, saying, "We're watching a movie, Hart. No working during the movie."

"But I work best with the TV on. You won't even notice I'm working." She reached again for the paper he had put on the coffee table.

He threw an arm over her shoulder and pulled her back. She was encircled in Max Valentine's arms! Della forced herself to relax and enjoy the movie. As it started, she'd tried to get into it, but his hand was touching her arm, and the other hand had grabbed hers.

Della leaned her head into him with a soft sigh. The movie was incredibly boring, and the characters didn't seem real. She tuned it out and started to let her mind wander to a case she was working on. Within minutes she felt Max's body relax—he had fallen asleep. She wanted to feel tired while cuddled up next to him in his arms, but she was wide awake.

After a minute or two, Della wiggled herself free and, without waking him, grabbed her computer and quietly started working. She some time every and every now and then she stopped typing just to just gaze at him. He was so cute when he slept. *There's no way he's comfortable like that*, she thought to herself, smiling and shaking her head.

When the sun started to come up, she had gotten more work accomplished than she'd thought she would, given the circumstances. She was ahead for the day; that is until the day started. Then she'd be swamped again.

Leaving him sleeping, she went down to her bedroom to get ready. Her sisters were bound to call soon anyways since both were early risers. Zoey won the race to call Della first, but the call was short since Gabe got home from work, and Zoey had to go.

Della was sitting on her bed and talking to Evie when Max walked into the room. He had that "just woke up sexy" look, and it made her stomach clench. He smiled at her and walked into her bathroom, shutting the door. When he came out a few minutes later, she had ended the call with Evie and was just sitting on the edge of the bed.

"Morning," she said.

"You waited until I fell asleep and worked all night." He was onto her.

"Maybe. I told you I wasn't tired," she said as he walked over to her.

He was in front of her, so she stood up. Whatever he had to say, she would take him head-on. To her surprise, Max didn't say anything right away. He just took her face between his hands and looked at. "The bruise is going to be faint. I was terrified when I saw that man punch you, Della. I never want to see that again." Then he lowered his lips to her cheek, and she felt the feather-light touch of his lips on her.

Then with his hands, he shifted her face softly kissed her lips. He came in again, and Della met him halfway this time. By the third kiss, he had shifted her again so that he had better access to her mouth. Her response was to match him move for move. Their first kiss had surprised her, but her body was now responding with everything it had. By the time she felt his tongue slip into her mouth, she had gathered his shirt into her fists and was holding him close.

If they kept this up, her knees weren't going to last much longer. They were already weak and rubbery. Max groaned into her mouth and leaned forward into her, encouraging Della to pull him even closer. They were about to fall backwards on the bed when a loud buzzing shattered the silence. Reluctantly pulling her mouth from his, she hissed, "Shit." The bell rang again, and Della looked at the clock. It was barely seven. It could only be Jasper and the stuff Evie was sending.

Letting go of his shirt, she smoothed it with her hands, then pulled away from him. The doorbell rang again, and Della groaned. As she turned away, she swore she could hear Max chuckling behind her. Stomping down the stairs, she looked through the peephole and saw her brother-in-law. She opened the door and greeted him. "Hey, Jasper."

"I was told to look at you and make sure you're okay." He said, nonchalant. "She said I better check for broken bones, but I won't."

She grabbed the box he was holding. "You saw me, so tell her I'm fine."

"I will. Glad you're okay this time." Jasper smiled, then turned and left.

Stalking back up the stairs with the box, she went to her office instead of the bedroom. There was no way she would be going back in there with Max Valentine. They would probably end up finishing what they had started.

"What did you get?" Max said as he walked in the office a moment later, not mentioning the kiss.

"Looks like bread and cookies … and a box of cherry tomatoes. She took out all the weird extras she usually sends," she replied, not mentioning the kiss either. Unfortunately for her, it was the only thing on her mind.

"Looks good except for the tomatoes."

Was she just going to go on with life and act like she didn't kiss Max Valentine? If he was going to pretend it didn't happen, she could play that game.

Taking the tomatoes out of the box, she carried the rest over to Max and said, "You can bring these to Sally and Mae."

"But they're yours."

"Trust me, I get them all the time. You enjoy these." She looked into his eyes, trying to see if he was thinking about the kiss. Probably not.

"I have to get ready for work. Bring the shirt back later, and I'll wash it for Chad." She dismissed him, hoping he would just leave.

"Can we talk about it?" he asked from the doorway, still holding the box.

Della looked up at him. *Nope, not going there.* "I can talk to Chad if you want to keep the shirt. It's from his last band, so maybe he would be okay with parting with it."

"I mean about the kiss. I want to kiss you again," he replied, staring at her lips.

"No, you can't." She lied, not wanting to admit how much she loved it. Her lips were still tingling, and it had happened forever ago.

"Liar," he said with a grin. He turned and walked out of her office and down the hall. Max stopped on the landing of the stairway and hollered, "I'll be kissing you again, Della Hart."

His footsteps pounded down the stairs, and then she heard her front door slam shut. At the sound, she fell across her couch, then pulled the blanket over her head and groaned. That man was going to be the death of her. He was going to burn her up with that mouth of his.

CHAPTER 10

It HAD BEEN two days since Max had kissed Della, and for two days, he hadn't seen her. Either she hadn't ventured out of her house, or she had gone somewhere without him noticing. His book was taking a backseat to him watching for Della. That was nothing new since writing his book took a back seat to almost everything.

Today was the first day Max had started thinking maybe he needed a job. The chances of getting this book written were not very high, so maybe he should be working on his resume. He could probably work for Della; she certainly needed help. Then he could see her every day.

Her front door had stayed shut all day—Chad hadn't even come to work. Yesterday he'd spent the day painting, and Sally had spent the day on the porch. Today it was his turn to sit on the porch and wait for a sighting at the mansion.

Max had waited for her to enter her upstairs office, but the light hadn't turned on. Maybe she had stayed out at one of her sister's places. He had even watched as Chad installed blinds late in the day from his desk.

The blinds were a little annoying, but he smiled and wondered why he had never noticed he could see right into the room across from him. Now that he knew he could see into her lair, he checked for her all the time. It had dawned on him when he was trying to write later that day that she had been watching him when she'd offered the fan. She could see the heat was getting to him.

After putting in three hours of watching for her while pretending to read a book, a big pickup with a trailer pulled up in front of the mansion. When it stopped, he could see the driver was her blonde sister, recognizing her from the picture beside Della's bed. The trailer said "Hart Farms" in bold letters. Suddenly, Max realized that it was Saturday. Della must have been at the farmer's market in Minneapolis. The pickup pulled away right as Della started up the steps, wearing red leggings and high heels again. They looked great on her as she unlocked her front door.

Slamming his book shut and laying it on the swing, he grabbed the shirt he had been carrying around for days and headed to her house, telling himself he must hurry because he didn't want her to have to come back downstairs, not because he was excited to see her again.

Max jammed his finger into the doorbell and waited for her to answer. After a few minutes, he rang it again. And waited again. Was she seriously not going to open the door? Was she going to ignore him? Again, he rang the bell.

The door opened, and Della pursed her lips at him. "What do you want, Valentine?"

He held up the shirt in front of him. "I brought the shirt back."

She waved her hand in dismissal. "Chad said you can keep it."

"I don't want it, so I'm returning it." He insisted, shoving it into her hand.

She grabbed it from him with a huff. "Thank you."

Della started to close the door, and he put his foot out to block it. "Can we talk?"

"No, you said I would never have to talk to you again," she reminded him of the farmer's market weeks before.

"I changed my mind," he said.

Swinging the door open wide, she replied, "You can talk while I eat, and then you leave. I need a shower and some sleep."

She walked away from him towards the kitchen. It wasn't a bad view. He had caught up to her by the time they made it to the kitchen. Max took her shoulders in his hands and shifted her towards the stools. "You sit, and I'll make you something."

She went more willingly than he had expected. As he looked through the fridge for something to cook, he realized she had very little to eat in here. Mostly vegetables. Opening the freezer, it was full of frozen packages of meat. Turning to look at her, he saw her head resting in her folded arms. "What do you want me to make?"

Her head came up. "Cereal."

"Cereal it is." He started opening cabinets to find the cereal and bowls. When he found them, he brought them to the counter for her. She poured herself a bowl as he grabbed the milk. After trading her a spoon for the milk, he asked, "Long day?"

"Evie got on my last nerve, and then she started working on that one," she answered around bites.

"Sounds like a fun day in the sun."

"It was brutal."

"Sally and Mae say thank you for the goodies. They were delighted," he said, smiling.

"I love those two. What did they fight about today? Chad has Saturdays off," she asked.

"I don't remember. It was about people I've never heard of. Sally told me something the first day I got here, and it'd been stuck in my head ever since." He watched her as she ate.

"What, that I'm fascinating?" Her eyebrow went up in question.

"It was 'fetching,' and yes, you are. But no, it was something else," he said. "She said that they fight every day, but it makes their relationship stronger."

Della put the bowl down and dramatically held her hand over her chest. "That is beautiful. So romantic."

He looked at her skeptically. "Romantic?"

She nodded, hand still on her chest. "They're still so happy after all these years."

"Yeah, they're happy." He agreed, even though they fought, they were happy with each other's company.

"Are you still in the dark over there, Valentine? That's the most romantic thing ever said, and you're blind," she said laughing and shaking her head.

"I have no idea what you are talking about." He was getting tired of her vague hints that lead nowhere.

Della gave him a flat look. "Max, they're not sisters."

"Then what are they?"

"Two ladies sharing a house for over fifty years." Della raised an eyebrow.

His face was a mask of confusion. "Roommates?"

"Really, Valentine? Really? They're lovers!"

"What? No, they aren't," he said, but the pieces all fell neatly into place.

"Yes, Valentine. *Lovers*." Della was laughing at him.

"But Chad … Sally loves Chad," he argued.

She just laughed louder. "So it can't be true because Sally appreciates a young body to look at."

So many conversations fell into place, and he started to laugh as well. "They think you are pretty good-looking. Mae asks about you almost every day."

Della got up and put her bowl in the sink and shrugged. "I am very attractive to a certain set."

At some point while she'd been sitting, she had taken off her shoes, and she was now a good four inches shorter than when she had sat down. He wanted to grab her into his arms but instead said, "You're very attractive to another set also."

"Don't go there, Valentine. I'm not up for this banter of yours today," she warned.

"Okay, okay. I'll stop trying to get in your pants." Max put his hands in the air in surrender, and he was relieved when he heard her quiet laugh before she turned around.

"At least for today. You can resume tomorrow if you want." She leaned against the sink, looking at him. "Thanks for making me laugh, I needed it. Evie has been putting pressure on me to talk, but I don't want to talk right now. Probably never. She just won't let up."

"I'm sorry. You look tired," he said, wanting to hug her and not let go until she felt better.

"I'm tired. I just want to shower and crawl into bed. You go back to your writing," she replied, stifling a yawn.

"I'm having a hard time with that, honestly." He admitted to someone for the first time.

"How far are you?" she asked.

Max folded his arms over his chest, a little embarrassed. "I'm having trouble with the beginning."

"So, you haven't done anything. All those hours you've been sitting there, and nothing?" she asked in disbelief.

"Yeah, writer's block."

"What the book about?"

"The mob?"

"Whole thing or just one guy?"

"Each chapter's about a different guy."

"Start with your chapters, then end with the beginning. By the time you've written it all, you'll probably know how to start it. It's like a complicated merger, start at the end and work your way back to the beginning," she suggested. Even though she looked exhausted, her mind was as sharp as ever. She was still the one with all the answers.

He walked over to her and slowly put his arms around her; she needed a hug more than anything right now. Feeling her melt into him, Max just held her. When she pulled away, he kissed her forehead and let her go. "I'm going to start on chapter one. You are brilliant, now go. I'll clean up in here and let myself out."

Turning her around, he gently pushed her towards the door, patting her butt as she walked away. He watched her walk through her office area, and he was starting to think that a day with her sister had left her in worse condition than a punch to the face.

After putting the cereal boxes away and washing her bowl and spoon, he lingered in the old kitchen, listening to the water run through the pipes above him. He couldn't help but visualize her in the shower. All he wanted to do was climb those stairs and join her, but she would rip him to shreds if he didn't leave her alone when she asked.

Walking out the front door, he knew she had just broken through his writer block, and it had taken her two seconds. Again, he wished he would have noticed her ten years ago. He'd wasted so many years without her in his life, and now he didn't know how he was going to walk away from her when his book was done.

CHAPTER 11

A TEXT WOKE DELLA. Not one, but six. All were from Zoey, and all were about how Evie was in such a bad mood. She wanted to know what had happened in Minneapolis. Della wanted to ignore them, all six of them, but if she did Zoey would call.

Della: Evie's digging into my business, and I told her to get her nose out of my life. She took it exactly like I wanted her to.

Any hope of going back to bed was now gone for Della, and she hadn't even slept for three hours. Maybe by morning, she would catch another hour or so. Throwing off the covers, she grabbed her phone and headed down the hall. Now that she was awake, she might as well get some work done.

Zoey: You and Evie are keeping secrets from me.

Della rolled her eyes at the message. It had been better when it was her secret alone; Evie was driving her crazy. From the moment she had picked Della up at five in the morning, Evie was on her for more details about her past.

She'd told Evie over and over that she didn't want to talk about it, but Evie just kept bringing it up, and the questions kept coming all day. Who? Where? When? How? Della had answered nothing. By the time they were driving home, she once again trapped in the pickup, and Evie just wouldn't take the hint.

By the time they had made it halfway home, Della had finally had enough and had told her sister that she would never talk about it with her. Evie knew as much as she did, and that was all she would ever know. Della just wished she had never told her sister about it in the first place.

After that, neither sister had spoken another word. When Evie had finally dropped her off, they didn't even say goodbye. Della had never been so relieved to be away from one of her two favorite people, and she didn't know if she wanted to see her anytime soon.

She had known it was Max when the doorbell went off. She had been able to ignore him for almost two days. After her day with Evie, though, she wasn't up for seeing Max. She had no strength to fend off his advances.

But then in true Max fashion, he'd lifted her spirits and made her laugh. His hug had made a lot of the pain of the day melt away; actually, it did more for her than the shower she later took.

Max, she thought and looked at the blinds on her windows. They were blocking her view to his bedroom. She curled up on her couch and pulled a blanket over her. *Better keep those shut since he was top on her mind tonight.*

Picking up her phone, she typed back to Zoey.

Della: It's not about you. It's all in the past and should stay there. I'm going to bed now. Goodnight.

Now her sister would leave her alone. Evie wouldn't text. If she had anything to say, she would've said it in the car. Della wouldn't speak to her even if she did call.

Pulling her laptop to her and grabbing some files from the coffee table, she opened the file she had been working on last night. Another woman in this town had lost most of her custody of her kids in the last few years, only to then end up with them full-time but with no child support from the father. The theme seemed to run through most of the cases she had been working on for the last six months. The man would get the kids and all the assets, and then he would just leave the kids with their mother because he never really wanted the kids in the first place. So, the mother was left with nothing but mouths to feed and no one to help.

There were now three lawyers in this town, and she was the only one who cared about these women. She saw the other lawyers' names show up in all her case filings. Their names were interchangeable. They were the same.

Della knew she could argue all these cases and get these women both custody and child support anywhere in this country, but not in this county. Their county had two judges, and both were chauvinistic jerks. They had been judges since she was young, and neither thought much of her or her clients. She was learning her clients would never get fair trials in this county.

Her first month open, a woman had come into the office bruised and battered, scared to death of her husband, and needing out. Della had sat the woman down in her office and told the woman to go to a shelter in Minneapolis, find a lawyer there, establish residency, and then start the divorce process. Since then, she'd sent more women along that same route, knowing they would never get out if they stayed in this town.

As she typed, her phone buzzed with a text. She wanted to ignore it but, she was a glutton for punishment and looked at it anyway.

Max: Are you working? I can't see you.

Max's message made her smile. The new blinds were closed, so she couldn't see him either.

Queen of Harts: Yes.
Max: Can I come and work with you?
Queen of Harts: Door's unlocked.

Within minutes she heard the door open and close downstairs. Della listened as his footsteps came up the stairs and down the hall. Then, like magic, he was there in her office with her. He was wearing black basketball shorts and a red t-shirt. The man looked good in anything.

"Hi," he said brightly.

"Hi," she answered back.

She watched him sit down and put his laptop and papers down on the coffee table. He turned to her and saw that she was wrapped up in her blanket, then smiled at her mischievously. With one finger, he pulled at the blanket until it loosened a few inches, then quickly peeked inside.

"You're not naked." Max frowned, sounding a little disappointed.

She giggled. "Maybe next time."

"Do you have another one of those?" He let his hand trail down the soft blanket, brushing her breast has he did.

"No," she answered. "Just this one. I can go get the one off the bed, so you have a blanket too."

He pulled her closer to him. "No, we can share this one if you're not way over there."

Watching as he rearranged the blanket around them, she felt his side pressed against hers, and he was hot. His heat was engulfing her, and the blanket wasn't helping.

As she settled her laptop on her lap and watched as he did the same, she whispered, "You're hot."

"Thank you." He turned and planted a kiss on her forehead.

"Not that." She pushed her body against his. "There's heat drifting off you."

"I live in an oven, and your house is cold."

"I like it this way. How's the book?" She changed the subject, not wanting to talk about his hot body. That didn't matter, though; she knew she would still be thinking about it.

"Good. I've been typing since I talked to you. You *are* brilliant, you know that? I had never thought about not starting in the beginning," he said.

"I'm glad you were finally able to start it. You have ten pages already?" She didn't want to look at his screen, but they were so close, and she couldn't help it.

"Yep, and it's been writing itself," he replied happily.

"You just know the material so well that it feels like it."

After that, they fell into silence as they both dug into their own work, Max typing and once in a while, looking up something in the file of papers he brought while Della mostly looked through her papers and sometimes typed. Hating to move from his side, she had to get some files from downstairs, so she set her computer on the coffee table and got up.

Max looked up from his computer. "Where are you going?"

"I need a few files. Do you want something to drink?" she asked, realizing he had been there an hour, and she hadn't offered. She wasn't a great host.

"No, I'm good. Come back soon."

Walking down the stairs into the darkness, Della wondered if she could keep Max at arm's length much longer. When he was around, all she wanted to do was kiss his smart mouth, and knowing how good he was with his mouth, she knew it wouldn't end with just a kiss next time.

After grabbing the files she had come down for, she picked up a couple more on a hunch. Heading back up, she realized she should've grabbed a few more, so she dropped those off and went back down. After carrying up another dozen or so, she set them on the coffee table in a neat pile. Della didn't snuggle back in next to Max. Instead, she sat perched on the edge of the couch, opening one file after another.

So engrossed in her work, she almost didn't notice when Max ran a hand down her spine. If the touch hadn't left tiny sparks of electricity in its wake, she wouldn't have been aware.

"What are you doing?" he asked, moving closer to her.

"Looking at these files. These are all files of clients who want to get their child arrangements changed. These are the two lawyers in town; they used to be the only ones. Over here are clients with out-of-town lawyers." She was pointing to a yellow legal pad she had been writing on.

"This column is the clients' names. See no lawyer from another town has ever even won a case here in town, not even close. It's as if hiring a better lawyer is just asking to loss everything. Two women even had to pay their ex's legal fees. But look at the rest. There's a pattern here; I just can't see it," she said, tapping the legal pad. Della leaned against the couch and shut her eyes, letting her mind wander.

"I don't see it, but this Keller guy gets a lot of the wives."

"He's a complete ass. He likes to think most of the women will sleep with him." Gabe had told her that early on. It was disgusting.

"Sleazy," Max said, frowning.

"It is. Williams doesn't try to get in your pants but treats you like you're the problem because nobody should leave their husband, no matter how bad it gets." She rolled her eyes. "And don't get me started on the judges. Those pricks hate me."

Della squeezed her eyes shut against the memory of one of them calling her 'little lady,' in open court last week. Both judges used little demeaning comments about her that would end up in official documents.

"I suppose because you're a woman? And an educated one?" he asked.

"You've met them, and besides, I represent women, which means I'm screwed in this town." The thought had been floating in the back of her mind for months. Saying it out loud made it feel real, though.

"Maybe you have to hire some lady lawyers to join you. More are graduating every year."

"Why would a young lawyer want to come to Birch Cove?" she asked, popping open an eye to see his face.

"Because she wouldn't have to work eighteen-hour days, and she wouldn't have to do all the work for others for years before getting cases of her own. She can afford a house of her own. If she had a family, she would have time to spend with them. It would be so much better than Rodgers and Associates. They'd finally get a fair shake," he said.

She had opened both eyes and was looking at him. She had never thought of bringing on another lawyer or two. There would be enough work.

"But no matter how many good lawyers there are, the judges suck," she replied sadly.

Max shrugged. "Then you have to become a judge."

"What? Me be a judge? I'm not old enough yet." She stumbled over the words.

"Yes, Della Hart, a judge."

"No, I wouldn't make a good judge yet. I need to be a lawyer for a few more years," she insisted.

Max smiled at her. "You'd make a great judge."

"I thought you said I was a great lawyer?"

"And that's what will make you a great judge. You know the law better than anyone I know."

The crazy thought started playing out in her mind. A judge? Her? Now? Maybe in fifteen years, but certainly not now. Could she do it? Maybe she should concentrate on hiring another lawyer. Her mind was racing with all the things she would need to do for that.

Max stood up and held out his hand. "Della."

Looking up, she smiled and took his hand, and he brought her to her feet. Letting go of her hand, his arms went around her waist and he whispered, "I'm going to kiss you again."

Looking into his gray eyes, she whispered back, "I'm going to kiss you back."

Max smiled and whispered back, his mouth hovering over hers. "I'm not going to stop with just a kiss."

"I hope to God not. Maybe this should start down the hall—"

Before she had the words out of her mouth, he had scooped her up and into his arms and was carrying her down to her room. When he set her down, she was shaking with nervous energy and excitement.

His arms went back around her and were holding her butt, clamping her against his obvious erection. When he had set her down, she had grabbed at his shirt, clenching it in her hands. Watching him lower his head to hers, she pulled back a little. "No strings, right? Just fun."

A grin pulled at his mouth as he said, "And you say I'm the playboy." His mouth lowered to hers again.

"Valentine." She pulled back again, and he stopped.

"No strings, Delphinea."

Bouncing up on her toes, her mouth finally met his. His lips were warm and soft as she started kissing him, but they soon turned hot and demanding after just a moment. When his tongue slid into her mouth, she was ready for it and matched his passion. She was so caught up with kissing him, she was surprised when his hands cupped her breasts. Moaning, Della arched her back, pushing them fully into his hands.

An involuntary whine came from her throat when his mouth left hers, but his mouth had found her neck, so she tipped her head to give him better access to the delicate skin. With a tug, she pulled his shirt up and then over his head. Even though she'd seen him shirtless many times in the last few weeks, she still wanted to see him now. Pushing him away, she said, "I want to see you, Max Valentine."

Glorious, she thought as her hands ran over his abs and up his chest. The light from the hallway was the only light in the room, and it was barely enough. But there was no way she was going to stop touching him to turn on a light.

As she looked and felt his body, he pulled her top over her head, her arms falling away from his chest as he did. When she lowered them again, he was already bent down, taking a taut nipple into his mouth. Della watched him work in the dim light, sliding her hands into his hair. She loved the feeling of his chocolate hair between her fingers, and she caressed his head as she held him tight to her breast. Max softly bit down on her nipple, and she arched her back in response, moaning at the explosion of pleasure coursing through her body.

As Max moved to her other breast, she felt his hand trail down her side and slip into her loose-fitting lounge pants. Della quickly pulled her hands away from his head and pushed her pants and underwear down as far as she could, then slowly, he brought them lower until they were in a puddle at her feet. Feeling his hand slide up the inside of her leg, she grabbed his head again, making sure he didn't stop suckling her breast. Knowing what was coming, his name left her mouth as he cupped her mound. "Max, yes."

As his fingers found the center of her core, she started rocking her hips with his movements. His mouth pulled away from her breast, and she knew he was looking at her. but she didn't care. All she cared about was how he was making her feel. Her orgasm was coming fast, and she wasn't going to be able to stand through it, "Max, I'm going to fall."

And fall, she did, knocking them both to the floor and onto her soft rug. She was lying on top of him. There was no laughing at the situation because her body was still rolling with the orgasm. Della pulled him on top of her with all the strength she had and said, "Now. I need you inside me now."

She reached for his shorts to get them off, but her arms were too short. She was getting angry at her shortness and wanted him naked. "Max, *please.*"

Della felt his movements as he shrugged off his shorts, pulling out a condom from one of the pockets. He'd started opening it when she grabbed it from him and said, "I'm on the pill. Just get inside me *now.*"

Stopping, Max looked into her eyes, and she smiled. Suddenly, she felt him plunge into her body, causing her breath to hitch as she looked down between them. Max tilted her chin up so that their eyes met again, and a moan tore through her. When he started moving, it was fast, and she never wanted it to stop. Digging her fingers into his back, she chanted his name in rhythm with their bodies.

Della's climax was coming fast, but she wanted more time with him. Her body demanded release, and she could do nothing but appease it as she went over the edge, feeling him follow her.

The floor was hard below her back, and Max's body was hard as he lay on top of her. She was in a rock sandwich and never wanted to move again. She, Della Connor Hart, had just had sex with Max Valentine.

With her hands lazily running up and down his back, she said, "You're pretty good at that."

Max lifted his head, then rested it on her chest. "You're not bad yourself, Hart."

"We didn't make it to the bed." She chuckled as she reached up and touched the bedspread above them.

"I guess we'll have to do it again."

He rolled them, so she was on top and he was on the floor. Slowly, she got up from his body and climbed into the bed that had been so close, but so far away. He got up and followed her. She stopped him and said, "This is my side. I already told you that."

Motioning him to go to the other side, she was rewarded by watching him slowly walk naked to the other side of the bed, giving her a show. He was as amazing as she'd always thought he would be. Max Valentine was gorgeous and hers, at least for now.

Climbing into bed across from her, he smirked and looked at her closely. Then he pulled her to him so that they were face to face, body to body, and just lying there. Starting at the top of her head, his hand began exploring her body. Hair, neck, face, shoulders, he was caressing her as if he were trying to memorize her body. "Where's the tattoo?" his voice was husky as he asked.

Della pulled the sheet down so that it was barely covering her hips. The tattoo was on her side, usually hidden by her bra strap. There were three hearts, two red, and one outlined in red. They were connected, but barely. Each was about the size of a nickel.

He ran his hand over the ink, then he leaned over and kissed the first heart, then laid back down. "I assume the first one represents you."

"The other two are my sisters. Evie's isn't red because she doesn't have red hair."

"And you got this when you had an office right next to me?" he asked in disbelief.

"I did a lot of things without you noticing," she whispered, not wanting to talk about her life before.

Max traced a finger around her tattoo, then trailed up her side and to her breasts. "Do you do a lot of no-strings relationships?"

Sitting up and turning to get out the bed, she said, "Sometimes, I like sex but don't want a relationship. I'm not the marriage and kid's kind of person."

His hand shot out and grabbed her arm as he answered, "I don't know if I'm a marriage and kid's person either. I've never thought about settling down with a woman."

"You don't have to say that because I did," she replied flatly.

"I'm not. Don't get defensive, so I get mad and leave. I know your tricks, Della. You've played them on me too many times." He called her out.

"I'm sorry. You're the first to figure it out." She admitted out loud. Nobody had ever called her out on her biggest move to get out of emotional situations.

Max kissed her forehead. "Don't be sorry, Della, just don't do it again. We can have a conversation about it."

"Okay, a conversation." She agreed.

"This was not a one-time thing. I'm going to have sex with you again," he whispered.

She turned to look at him. Was he kidding? He thought this could be a one-time thing? "The agreement was no relationship, Max. I want to have sex with you until you go back." He wanted the truth, and she was going to give it to him.

Max dramatically rolled his eyes as if their arrangement had been obvious. "Agreed, and I want to have sex with you again now."

Laughing at his joke, she glanced down at his erection and saw it was ready for round two. Crawling across the bed, she straddled him and purred, "Can't have you waiting, can we?"

Nuzzling her neck, he pushed against her chest until her back was on the bed. He smiled down at her and said, "I need you flat on your back right away. Can't have you falling again."

Della reached out and finally touched his hard shaft with her hand. It was perfect; everything about him was perfect. As she caressed it, she whispered into his ear, "I just can't have an orgasm while standing yet."

Rewarded by his moan, she bit his ear lobe, then pulled it into her mouth. Before she knew what was happening, he had grabbed both her hands and was holding them above her head. She looked into his eyes as she grabbed his waist with her legs, pulling his penis towards her core.

"Della," he moaned as his shaft slid into her again, slower this time, but deeper.

She sighed in content as her hips set the pace. Their eyes caught as the rhythm soon increased with the need they both shared, locking together as they watched each other go over the edge. Afterwards, Max let go of her arms and pulled her to him. Her back was to his front.

Della found herself melting into his body. She had never slept with the men she had sex with over the years, mostly because she wasn't a big sleeper, but also because she had never felt this comfortable before. Soon, she drifted off, still sheltered in his arms.

CHAPTER 12

SUNDAY DAWNED bright and sunny in Della's bedroom, and Max woke up alone in the giant bed. Somehow, he knew he would, and it didn't bother him. He knew Della was nearby, probably down the hallway working. That woman could work.

Pulling on his shorts but leaving his shirt off, he wandered down the hallway to find her. There she was, no blankets or pajama's now, but dressed in designer jeans and a billowy, light gray shirt. File folders were spread out around her on the couch and coffee table.

Walking up behind her, he kissed the top of her head. "Find the pattern yet?"

She looked up at him and smiled. "No. It's there, though."

With her head tipped back, he kissed her lips and said, "Morning."

"Morning."

"Have you been up long?" He walked to the other side of the couch.

"I didn't go back to sleep after the shower. I don't need that much sleep," she replied.

It had only been an hour or so after they had fallen asleep when she woke him up and asked if he wanted to take a shower. He agreed, and they had stayed in the shower until the warm water turned to ice.

After wrapping her into a towel, he carried her back to the bed and finished what they had started in the bathroom. It hadn't taken him any time to fall asleep again, but not her.

Her attention was back on the papers in front of her. She was beautiful, and she had no idea. Just watching her flip through papers turned him on, and then his mind would stray back to how she had acted in bed, which made him want to drag her back there.

Glancing up, she saw the look in his eye and blushed. "No, I have to go out to Zoey's for lunch. I don't have time to rock your world."

He laughed. "That's not what I was thinking."

"Liar."

Max closed the file she was holding. "You're right. Can I go with you to your sister's?" he asked. He couldn't believe he hadn't met anyone in her family yet.

"No, it's a family day. I don't think you want to spend time with my family," she said firmly.

"But I can deflect Evie. She'd never talk to you about your business if you'd brought a man home with you." Why was he pushing about this? Did he really want to be drilled by her sisters about his intentions?

"It would give me a day away from her probing," Della agreed, pondering the idea.

Max looked like a cat that had just caught a mouse. Jumping up, he said, "I'll go shower and be back in fifteen minutes."

When he was heading out the door, she called after him, "Take your computer and papers!"

He stopped and smiled at her. "I'll just leave them here. That way, I'll have to come back tonight." Max winked at her, then ducked out the door.

An hour later, he was sitting in the passenger seat of her fancy SUV. The windows were rolled down, and the sunroof was open to the wind. His arm was draped over her seat, and he was rolling a red curl around his finger until the wind whipped it out of his grasp, then he started again.

"Let's go over this again. Who's married to the cop?" he asked. He knew the answer, but the closer they got, the tenser she was getting.

"Zoey's married to Gabe, and their baby is Connor. He's the boy baby," she replied.

"And Evie is married to …?"

"Jasper. He grew up next door, and his cousin Clementine might be there. She's thirteen now. Grandma Betty is his grandma. She was my grandma growing up since I didn't have any others after the Connors' died before I was six. Her husband Bill died last year."

He didn't know if touching her was stressing her out or not, but he kept it up. "Who's going to take me outside and give me the talk about treating you right?" He leaned over and nuzzled her ear.

"Evie since she pretends to be the oldest. That's her place, by the way." She pointed out his window as they drove by. All he saw was a cute house with a lot of gardens in the yard.

"Nice," he said as they turned into the next driveway. They were the first to arrive, judging by the lack of cars in the yard.

"Max, my family makes fun of each other all the time. I just want you to know that. It's what they do, but they don't do it to be mean," she said as the car stopped.

"That's where you get your sarcastic whit, huh?" He touched his index finger to her nose.

She looked nervously at the house. "Yes, and they're all here."

"Did they walk?" he asked, looking around at the empty yard again.

"Yep." Then Della opened her door as the front door flew open, and a large group of people came pouring out of the house.

Slowly getting out of the car and walking around it, he watched as everyone got a hug from her, some full-on, and some with one arm. It was like they never saw each other, and Della had come for her yearly visit, not the weekly one.

As the hugging settled down, people started to notice Max standing by the car. Della walked back to him and grabbed his hand, pulling him to the crowd. "Everybody, this is Max, Mae's nephew. I invited him to lunch today."

Della's twin walked up to him and said, "I'm Zoey. Do they share a bedroom?"

Max smiled at her. Upon closer inspection, he could tell them apart instantly. Zoey had a wild energy that Della didn't have. It practically vibrated out of the younger woman. "No, Mae sleeps in the master bedroom, and Sally sleeps in the bedroom next door."

Zoey face broke out into a conspiratorial grin. "I bet there's a door between their rooms."

The blond walked up to him and Della, and Max wrapped his arms around Della who was in front of him, hoping it would help ease the tension the blonde brought. Evie said, "Never mind her. I'm Evie. I am married to Jasper, the dark-haired, good-looking one."

"Hey everyone. This guy must be Ben," Max greeted them all and turned to the half-grown kid who was taller than all the sisters.

The sandy-haired boy walked up to him and held his hand out. Max took the hand and shook it, "Ben Hart. Max? What's your last name?"

"I'm Max Valentine," he said, letting the boy's hand go.

Zoey broke out laughing. Turning, Max looked at her. "Hart, Valentine. If you get married, Della can't hyphenate her name."

The entire group broke out laughing except him and Della. He knew she wasn't laughing because they really weren't in a relationship. Max wasn't laughing simply because it had never dawned on him what their names together would be. He kissed Della's head and said, "Della won't be changing her name, so I'll have to become Valentine-Hart. That has a ring to it, no?"

Relief washed over him when he felt her laugh in his arms. The tension was averted—until Evie opened her mouth.

"Della should just change her name. She's just being stubborn not to," the blonde said.

Feeling Della tense in his arms, he gave her a quick squeeze and said, "I don't think we're at the name-changing stage of things, so let's just let it go."

Zoey jumped in. "Let's go inside. I have a few questions for Mr. Valentine. Do you get discounts around your holiday?"

Smiling, he followed her, taking Della's hand in his as they went. "No, I get nothing."

"Too bad. And you went through all that work to make a holiday too," Zoey replied.

As the group entered the house, the men seemed to stay in the living room as the women went to the kitchen. Since Della didn't let go of his hand, he went into the kitchen as well. He was here for her, and he would do everything in his power to make sure she was comfortable today.

He sat down on a barstool at the counter, and Della sat down next to him. She even put her hand on his leg, and he put his on top of it.

"So how long has this been going on?" Evie asked.

"Long enough," Della said, not answering.

Evie looked back and forth between Della and Max. "What does that mean?"

"It means that I didn't ask you about Jasper. Not even when you showed up pregnant a few months later," Della whispered at her sister. Their eyes never left each other's.

"No dirty laundry in front of my guest!" Zoey said to her sisters, shooing them away from each other. "Max, where are you from?"

"Minneapolis, born and raised."

Zoey smiled, and her energy was contagious. "What do you do?"

"I'm a lawyer, but I'm currently writing a book."

"A book, that's right. She's a lawyer too." Zoey gestured with her thumb at Della.

Max laughed. "I know."

"Do you know where her tattoo is?" Zoey asked innocently.

Max suppressed a grin at Zoey's pointed question, then raised an eyebrow at her. "Which one?"

Shocked, Zoey's face whipped to her sister. "When did you get another, and why didn't you let me go with? I want another one!"

Della got the joke and started laughing, "Zoey, I only have the one. He's just messing with you. And you almost passed out during your first one."

Zoey pouted for a second. "Well, he shouldn't."

"Did you get one past my wife, Max?" Gabe came into the room.

"I think so," Max stated.

"Good, she always thinks she's so clever," Gabe said as he wrapped his arms around Zoey.

"She *is* pretty clever." Zoey leaned into her husband.

"Never mind them," Evie said. "How long are you in Birch Cove, Max?"

"Until I finish my book."

"Don't you have to work?" She asked a little less subtly then her sister had.

"Not really. I have money saved, and my father left me quite a bit when he passed away. Not mansion money, but money," he replied. He and Della had never talked about money, but now she would know.

"Della doesn't have any." Evie pointed out, trying to act innocent when she'd made the comment.

"Good thing I have enough for the both of us," he quipped, smiling brightly at Della's nosy sister.

"Evie, if you're going to treat Max like this, we can leave," Della said calmly.

Jasper walked into the tense kitchen and said, "Evangelina, leave her alone. Della doesn't need your approval, and you never asked for hers."

Evie looked at Della and then to Jasper and sighed. "Okay, your right."

Jasper smiled and added. "I'm going to take my beautiful wife for a walk. Don't come looking for us."

Max watched as Jasper took Evie's hand in his and lifted it to his mouth to kiss it. Then turned and walked out of the house, still holding hands. He wondered if Evie's mood would be better when they came back. He hoped so.

"Well, okay," Zoey commented as they left. Then she turned to her sister. "One day, you'll tell me what you two aren't talking about." Looking over at Max, she said, "And one day, you'll tell me where her other tattoo is."

"I wonder which secret you will learn first, Zoey," Max replied, and he was rewarded with a laugh from both sisters.

"Gabe, get the photo albums. It's naked baby picture time!" Zoey called to her husband, who'd disappeared. "Della never brings anyone home to us."

When he came back, he was carrying a photo album and handed it to his wife. When she took it out of his hands, she kissed him quickly on the mouth. Max loved how affectionate Della's family was.

Pictures from the girls' childhoods were sparse. There were many from when they were very young, and multiple baby pictures of each girl. Then they came across the first day of school shots, and Della looked tiny and scared for first grade.

They had been flipping through the pages for a few minutes when Evie and Jasper walked back into the house. Max was studying a picture of Della on her graduation day—a very young-looking graduate. "You were fifteen here?"

Looking at the picture she said, "I was a summer baby, so actually, I was still fourteen. It sounds better when you say fifteen, though."

"Always so modest." He hugged her from the side. "Is this your dad?"

Della looked at the picture he was pointing at. She was in a cap and gown, and her dad looked older than he actually had been. "Yes."

Zoey looked down at the picture. "He didn't give you a graduation party, did he?"

He barely heard Della say, "No."

"Me either. Evie was the only one to get one of those." Zoey pointed at the mentioned sister.

"She only got one because I organized it. I organized one for you too, Zoey," Della said.

"You didn't organize my party, Della. You were off in college," Evie replied.

"You think Dad organized it? He had no idea what to do. I ordered the cake and the buns, and I had you send out all the invitations. He only knew when to show up."

Evie shook her head. "I would have remembered that."

"I remember it. I went with Della to pick up the stuff that day. She paid for it too." Zoey defended her sister.

"Why did you organize Zoey's? I was here," Evie questioned.

"Greg." Was all Della had to say.

"He was dead by then." Evie folded her arms over her chest.

"Exactly. You had a small kid, and no one to help. It took you a while to be as together as you are, Evie," Della reminded her sister.

Zoey butted in. "It's a good thing I didn't graduate then."

"You got your diploma, Zoey Hart. You just missed the last month of school. Which was your fault anyway." Evie rolled her eyes.

Zoey dramatically threw her hands up in the air. "I was framed!"

"You were in the school," Della reminded her.

"I wasn't in the *science* room. I was in the math room," Zoey argued.

"Two doors down? Not a strong alibi." Della smiled.

Gabe wrapped his arms around his wife and said, "Max, Zoey blew up the school and got kicked out and sent to the Army."

"I did not blow up the school. It only blew out a window, and I was in the math room getting the answers to the test for the next day." Zoey defended, trying to get out of her husband's grasp.

"Not helping your case, Zoey. And I'm your lawyer, remember?" Della laughed.

"If there wasn't a baby crying right now, I would argue you into the ground on this, Della Hart." Zoey finally got free of her husband's arms and left the room.

"Still touchy about that, I see," Evie said.

Max took his time looking at Evie's graduation picture and then a blank page that was supposed to be Zoey's. Flipping to the back page, Max saw a school picture of a girl who had red, curly hair and blue eyes.

"Who is this?" he asked Della.

"I don't know. I've never seen this picture before." Della picked it up and looked at the back.

Evie leaned over and looked at it. "Gabe found it in Dad's closet when we were putting in the new floors. It was stuck to the wall or something."

Gabe took the baby from Zoey when she came in, carrying two. "It was stuck in the door frame."

"It's definitely a relative, but we don't know who. We keep it in case someone shows up," Evie said with a shrug.

"I'm guessing it's Dad's kid," Zoey added.

Della ran her hand over the picture. "Too much Connor in this one. Does Mom have any cousins? Maybe grandpa strayed."

Max took the picture, then put it back in the album and closed it. Pushing it away, he looked at the two couples in the kitchen, each cooing over babies. Max glanced at Della, who was also watching. She was tense again.

Climbing off the stool, he took her hand. "Show me where you grew up."

She smiled at him and said, "Sounds great.

Weaving their way through the couples, they exited the back door onto a small porch. Della pulled Max along at a near run despite the three-inch heels on her sandals. Coming to a stop where the lawn ended and a black field of dirt began, she said, "Many a shoe has seen its end in this dirt. This is Zoey's pumpkin patch. They're putting up a fence along here before the season begins. During pumpkin season, people actually drive out here to pick their own pumpkins."

He pulled her into his arms, not caring much about the green growth in the field beyond them, "Doesn't seem like much."

Smiling up at him she said, "It's huge."

She wiggled out of his arms and pulled him along, a bit slower now. They stopped at a large gray metal building. "Machine shop," she said, as if that explained everything he needed to know.

Sweeping her arms across the yard, she added, "The vegetable gardens. This is where your tomatoes came from."

Giving him a sly wink, she walked him over to one. Della reached down and pulled a small red tomato from a plant, then put it up to his mouth. "Take it," she said. After letting her put it between his lips, he wondered if he was supposed to eat it.

Around the tomato in his teeth, he replied, "I don't like tomatoes."

He watched her green eyes sparkle as she pulled his head down and put her lips over his, taking the tomato from his teeth with her tongue. As he wrapped his arms around her, the kiss ended, and he watched her bite into the juicy fruit. He groaned when it popped in her mouth. Quickly, he covered her mouth with his and kissed her, not caring that she tasted of tomatoes.

When he finally lifted his head, she whispered, "I thought you didn't like tomatoes."

"I might never say that again." He kissed her lightly again. Max wanted to strip her down right here in the open in front of her family.

"I knew I could convert you. Want to see the barn?" She took him by the hand again and started for the big structure nearby.

It was darker and cooler in the barn than he'd expected. The smell was awful, but he was willing to put up with it to be alone with Della. He had her backed into a large wood fence in a flash.

Before he could kiss her, she giggled and took his face in her hands. "Looking for a roll in the hay?"

He laughed and slid his hands under her gray shirt, capturing her breasts as he said, "When in Rome."

"Save it for tonight." Her eyes looked sternly into his eyes, but Max could tell she was trying not to give in.

"Only of you do that tomato trick for me again. I almost took you right there on the spot," he said, rubbing her nipple one more time before lowering his hands.

"You'll have to ask for some tomatoes when we leave." She let go of his face, but not before lightly kissing his lips.

"Oh, I'll bring back a whole box of them." He winked and pulled her away from the fence.

CHAPTER 13

By the time they made it back in the house after looking over more garden beds, the guys were standing over a grill, watching burgers cook. Leaving Max with them, Della bravely walked into the house to face her sisters. This was the first time she had ever introduced her family to a man she was dating, not that she and Max were *really* dating.

Neither sister was holding an infant when she walked into the kitchen. Evie was making a salad, and Zoey was gathering paper plates and cups. Sitting on the same chair she had sat in before, Della watched the two work.

Zoey smiled at her. "I like him."

"Everybody likes Max Valentine," Della agreed, opening the photo album that was still on the counter.

"I like him with you. I saw that kiss out there. *Hot*." Zoey emphasized the last word. Then pretended to fan herself with her hand.

"Do you think it's going to turn into something?" Evie asked pointedly.

"Don't get excited you two. It's just a summer fling. Once his book is done, he's going back to Minneapolis." Della explained to her sisters. As much fun as it has been it will not last.

"Maybe he will stay, and you guys will get married," Evie said.

Della closed the photo album in front of her and looked at her sister. "No, Evie, marriage isn't in my plans. This is not a relationship. We're just friends."

"It could be a relationship, Della," Evie argued.

Della narrowed her eyes. "No, Evie, it's just sex."

"'Just sex' can turn into 'just a baby.'" Evie stared at Della. "It happened to me."

Della got up from her stool, still staring Evie down. "It will not happen to me, so you can take that out of your mind."

"Stop it. Stop it right now," Zoey yelled, then threw the pile of paper plates at them.

One hit Della in the head, and a few hit her in the chest and stomach. Grabbing a handful of them off the counter where they had landed, Della threw them at Evie, "Tell her to stop! I shouldn't have come out here. I knew she wouldn't just let me live my life."

"Let her live her life the way she wants to," Zoey rounded on Evie. "We are her sisters! We are support staff for her life. Della gets to make all the decisions, and we are the ones who support her. It's up to her if she lets us help make those decisions."

"But sometimes she makes the wrong decisions," Evie whispered.

"I cannot change the past, Evie. I had to be able to let it go," Della whispered back. Walking around the counter, she pulled Evie into her arms for a hug. Zoey's arms went around them both as they all cried in the middle of the kitchen.

"We need to spend more time together, no kids," Zoey said. "Della should come with us to Minneapolis on Saturday."

Della sighed and pulled away from their embrace, "No, I have too much work to go to another farmer's market."

"You need help." Evie handed out tissues to her sisters.

"Evie, let her decide what she needs," Zoey warned.

Della took her tissue. "That's okay, I'm actually looking into hiring a few lawyers and an office manager."

"Do you have anybody in mind?" Zoey asked.

"No, but I have contacted a few professors at the law school to see if they know of anyone who's looking for a small-town gig."

"Sounds promising. How about an office manager? Are you going to post it in the paper?" Evie seemed happy that Della was getting help in one part of her life.

"I guess, but I don't know who would apply," Della replied as the back door opened, and the three men and Ben came into the house with the burgers.

"Apply for what?" asked Gabe.

"Della's hiring some office staff!" Zoey informed him as she kissed him.

"Security?" Jasper asked.

"Office manager. Know anyone?" Della asked Jasper, but her focus was on Max as he walked through the room.

"I think I might." Jasper nodded. "Do you remember my cousin Casey?"

"No," Della admitted sheepishly.

"Yes," Evie said, "He worked for Bill one summer, didn't he? That was a good summer."

Jasper looked at his wife and raised an eyebrow. "I'll have to find out about that summer."

"I only have eyes for you, Reed." Evie took his hand and kissed the back of it.

"Anyway, he got tired of working security at one of the big banks in Minneapolis and is looking for something different," Jasper said.

"Jasper, I need an office manager, not security," Della reminded him. Max had pulled her so that her back was now leaning against his chest, and his arms were wrapped around her, just beneath her breasts.

"You need both," Evie stated thoughtfully.

"Casey isn't an idiot; he can file and answer phones, but he can also keep you safe," Jasper said. "I'll have him send you a resume."

"Go ahead. Can't hurt to look at him."

"What happened to the plates? Why are they are all over the place?" Gabe asked as he put the plate of burgers on the counter.

Della looked at him. "Your wife."

"Looks like her work." He nodded. "Did she make everyone cry too?"

"Yes," Evie said and laughed.

By the time they sat down to eat, the burgers were cold, but Ben was the only one who complained about the temperature of the food. Everyone else just laughed at the boy's complaints.

Looking around the table, Della knew she was going to miss having someone at her side when Max left. It was easy to forget that he would be leaving one day when he was getting along so well with her family. Why did he have to fit in so well? How was her heart going to survive him leaving?

CHAPTER 14

THE INTERVIEW WAS OVER, and Della had laid her pen down. Max had only sat in on six of the interviews with lawyers that the university had set up, but already he knew she wasn't be impressed with the young man in front of them. She had set her pen down after asking only four of the twelve questions on her list. So far, she had only not laid her pen down once. If she stopped writing down their answers to her questions, she had lost interest.

Taking over, Max asked another question of the young man, but he was bored with the young man as well. They only had three candidates left, and Della had wanted to hire two or three people. Things were not looking good.

Max let his mind drift as the young man talked about his achievements. It had been almost three weeks since he and Della had made love for the first time. Since then, he had practically moved into her house with her, spending his days working on his book while she worked on the bottom floor. It was the first time he had ever lived with a woman, and he was enjoying it.

Their routine had been established in the first few days, and it rarely wavered. Monday thru Friday were workdays. He had actually gotten his entire book written and was editing it now. Della was busy as ever, taking on more and more clients. He usually went across the road to his aunt's house for a snack in the afternoon. After work, he made supper, and they ate together and talked about their day. After the dishes were done, they went up and worked more, her on the vast amount of paperwork her job entailed, and him on his book.

If she grew tired of working, she would quietly put her computer away, then take his away from him so she could climb onto his lap and kiss him. He loved touching her as much as it seemed she loved touching him.

With luck, she would get some help at the firm so she could relax more. Maybe sleep more. Though she said she only needed a few hours of sleep a night, he wasn't convinced she wasn't working herself too hard.

The weekends were for family, and Della typically went out to the farms on Sunday. But Saturday, she spent with him. They went from making love to working to making love again all day. He loved it and looked forward to Saturday all week.

This Saturday, however, was being spent with young lawyers looking for a job. Watching Della ask another question about the future, he wondered what she thought of their future. They had agreed that this was a fling, nothing more, but Max didn't know how he was going to walk away from the woman. He had fallen in love with her over the summer. It was late July, and he was almost done with the book and didn't want to leave her.

Standing up, he shook the hand of the man and watched him leave the room. He and Della stayed standing, and Max glanced over her outfit, pencil skirt with a blazer over a pink shirt. The outfit was from her days at Rodgers and associates, but it didn't remind him of her when she was there.

They didn't talk about the candidate who had left the room; she only talked about them if they had impressed her. So far, they had talked little about the candidates.

"This is not going well." Della looked at the papers on her desk.

"Maybe the next one," Max said walking away from the table. "I'll go get her."

Walking to the hallway, he called out, "Lea Jeffery."

Heading back to the table, he didn't watch who followed him. As he walked across the floor, he watched Della's face and saw her eyebrow go up. Coming around take his seat again, he turned to see what had intrigued the redhead.

Lea Jeffery was tall, dark-haired, and older than anyone they had interviewed today. From the looks of it, her life had been harder than all the other candidates as well.

Della stood up and offered her hand, "I'm Della Connor Hart, and this is my friend, Max Valentine." Max stood and shook her hand also.

"Lea Jeffery, I pronounce the 'A' at the end," the woman said as she sat down in the chair across from them.

Della was reading through the resume again, so Max asked the first question. "Why do you want this job?"

The woman looked from one of them to the other and said, "Truth is, I want out of Minneapolis. I am tired of all the people. I don't want to spend all my time working. I have two kids, and I want to be able to spend time with them. I don't want to go to the office before they get up in the morning and stay until they go to bed."

Della looked up. She had yet to go off script all day, so Max was surprised when she asked, "How old are they?"

Lea relaxed when she heard the question. "Fifteen and twelve."

"You must've been young when you had them," Della commented.

"Yeah, and then it took a lot of time to get on my feet and back to school. Their dads haven't been involved at all."

"Are you divorced?" Della asked.

"No, never married," Lea answered honestly.

Max let them talk since he had no idea where Della was going with this. All he knew was that she was interested in this one. Unless something went very wrong, Lea already had the job.

"What kinds of jobs did you do before you went to school or during?" Della asked.

"A lot of waitressing. I did customer service at one of those phone banks, and I drove taxi for a while. Nothing that really had anything to do with law," Lea admitted.

"You had a 4.0 all the way through?" Della wrote down something on her paper.

"Yes."

"Did you want to work in family law or corporate law?" Della asked.

"Family. I've worked with social services over the years. I had some issues with my first's Dad's family for a while. I always wanted to help women and kids." Lea nodded.

"How would you handle it if a judge called you cupcake? You would be seeing the judge every week," Della asked. Max had no idea where that came from. What kind of judges did she go in front of?

"I would tell him I have a name, but since I would have to be in front of him every week, I would have to just let it go. I don't want my attitude to interfere in my clients' lives," Lea said.

"First you have to say, 'strike that from the record,'" Della told the woman. "Do you think you can handle that situation and many like it?"

"I think I can. It's a lot like waitressing." Lea smiled.

"You have the job if you want it." Della put down her pen.

"Della," Max said.

"Fine," she said, looking at him, "I will call you, Lea, in the next few days and offer you a job. We can discuss the particulars then."

"Really?" Lea asked.

"Yes. Max says not to hire you right now, but once I shake him, I'll call you. I think you'll work out perfectly. Take a few days and think about it; it's going to be a big change," Della said, standing to shake the other woman's hand.

"Thank you, Ms. Connor Hart," Lea replied as she accepted Della's hand.

"Just Della, please." She moved around the table to walk the woman out the door.

After the door had shut, Della said, "Finally! I knew it would be her. What did you think?"

"Does it matter? You hired her already," Max said but was smiling at her.

"No, I liked her. Judge Cramer is going to have a heart attack when that woman shows up in his courtroom. I am so excited!" Della said with a smirk on her face.

"How many judges call you cupcake?" He had to know.

"Just Judge Cramer. The other one calls me red." She had never told him much about the judges she argued in front of, just little bits and pieces.

"You can go to the governor with that. It's sexual harassment," Max said, frowning.

"I'm not going to make waves. Especially now that I think I'm running for judge. I really think I need to. I just need to get a few lawyers together for all the women in town," Della said, leaning over the table to look at the resumes in front of them.

"I think you should too." Max leaned over the table and kissed her. "I can see down your shirt when you lean like that. I like it."

He was surprised when she blushed at the comment. He had started to notice she was uncomfortable with compliments about her body. Unless they were actually getting physical, she was uncomfortable knowing he noticed her body.

"Let's talk to Casey and then the other two if they're still around," Della said, walking around the table and sitting down next to him.

Before he got up to get the man, he turned back to her. "Della Hart, I just want to say that you are beautiful. Inside and out."

He knew she would protest his compliment, so he put his hands over his ears and went to call in Casey. This time when he called Casey Armstrong, he looked at the man. He wasn't sure if it because Lea had surprised him or because this man could be working with Della every day.

Max had expected someone who looked like Jasper, but that was not this man. Casey was a few inches taller than Max, who was usually the tallest in the room, and his black hair was in a military haircut. The man was big and solid, the kind of guy you wanted on your side in a fight.

He was wearing a red polo shirt that was stretched tight over his chest and upper arms, showing only a small number of tattoos on his dark skin. After the man had sat down, Della leaned back in her chair.

"Casey Armstrong, Betty has told me to hire you. Should I?" *Another interview off the rails*, Max thought.

"If Aunt Betty says you should, then probably," Casey said with a grin.

"Can you type?" she asked.

He shrugged. "Some."

"File?"

"I know by ABC's." He smirked at his own joke.

"Answer phones?"

"Yes, I can.

"Schedule appointments?"

He shrugged again. "If I have something to write them in, yes."

"Why do you want to leave Minneapolis?" This was at last question on her list.

"My wife walked out on me over the winter, and I'm tired of all the people." His matter-of-fact attitude took Max by surprise.

"When did you work for Betty and Bill?" she asked.

"Summer before senior year. The next summer, I joined the Army."

"Are we the same age?" She tapped his resume.

"I think so. Thirty-three?" He shrugged again.

"Yes, for another a few days. So yes," Della said.

Max's ears perked up, he had no idea when her birthday was, and now, realized it was soon. Maybe he would talk to Zoey about when exactly it was. He and Evie were still not on good terms.

"I don't remember you. Charley had two kids, one a few years younger than me and the other was a lot younger."

"I was already in college and wasn't really going home in those days," Della admitted. Max didn't know she had been estranged from her family when she was young.

"That's why I don't remember you," Casey said, leaning back.

"You were at Bill's funeral?" she asked.

"Yeah, but I had to leave early. I had to work." He nodded.

"You didn't sit with the family," she pointed out.

"No, I brought my grandmother, and we sat in the back." He had an answer for it all.

"The wedding?" Della asked.

"It was during the day on a Friday." He shrugged yet again.

"I tried to tell them. They said it was Black Friday and that everyone would be off work. You missed frostbite." Della turned to Max and explained. "Evie and Jasper got married on the road between their farms during a blizzard. It was so cold. The minister didn't even do the vows or rings, just announced them married, and we all went to Betty's for the reception. It was very romantic, except the cold was awful."

"That's what grandma said." Casey grinned.

"Are you going to live with Betty or get a place of your own?" Della looked down at his application.

"If I get the job, I'll move in with Betty at first, then find something of my own," Casey said, looking a little surprised.

"Betty said to hire you, so I will. Family is family even when you have never met." Della got up and walked around the table. "I will give you a call in a few days to hammer out the details. I hope you can start soon. I need someone manning the office ASAP."

Casey stood and was well over a foot taller than Della, even with her heels on. Watching them shake hands, Max had to control himself from going around the table and getting between them. He wanted to prove she was his woman, and Casey had no chance with her. Jealousy had been eating him since the man had walked into the room.

Once again, Della walked him out of the room, and after shutting the door behind him, she gave him a thumbs up. As she back to the table, she frowned at him. "What's wrong with you? I hired an office manager."

Max shook his head. "I don't like him."

"Why?" She leaned into the table.

"He was not qualified." He leaned toward her.

"Maybe not, but there's nothing he can't learn, Max. He's Betty's nephew." She looked into his eyes.

"He was flirting with you."

"He was not!"

"I know what flirting is, and he was," Max argued.

"I think I would know if someone was flirting with me," Della exclaimed.

"No, Della, you don't. I flirted with you so much without you realizing," he explained. He had loved how she didn't realize it … until others flirted with her.

"I knew you were flirting, but you weren't flirting *with me*. You just can't control it sometimes," Della replied.

"I don't flirt with someone if I don't want to sleep with them." He stared at her green eyes intently.

"At the farmer's market, you flirted with me. You didn't want to sleep with me then." Della raised an eyebrow at him.

"I wanted to sleep with you when we met in the bar the night you got fired. I wanted to kiss you when you came back for your phone," he admitted, his voice growing husky. He didn't know why he was telling her this.

"I can't talk about this right now. Casey is family, nothing more." Della shook her head.

"You might have to tell him that," Max said as he went to let another candidate into the room. He wondered if she would ever notice how desirable she was. It wasn't even just her looks; it was her personality. After he talked to Della for a while, you realized how irresistible she was.

CHAPTER 15

WITH THE DAY'S interviews over, Max drove them to his apartment. Early in the week, when she had told him she would be doing interviews at the University today, he said they should stay at his place. She had felt stupid that she had forgotten he would have a place in Minneapolis; she didn't think of him living in Minneapolis anymore since he lived with her. But now they were walking down the hallway to his apartment.

Not knowing what to expect, once he opened the door, she would realize more about his personality and how he lived. She'd see how he would live after he left her. Della had dreamed of this moment for years, and now she was scared to see what was behind his door.

Stopping at his apartment, Max pulled out his keys and opened it, swinging the door wide. He motioned for her to enter first. The first thing she noticed was the modern furniture that occupied the entire apartment. The second thing was a massive row of windows facing the Mississippi River. Dropping her bag as she walked to them, she stood in front of the windows, staring out at the view before her.

While watching the summer sun bouncing off the buildings below her, she felt Max wrap his arms around her. She had worn her hair up today and was happy when his lips touched her bare neck and then slowly moved up to her ear.

"Beautiful," he whispered into her ear as his hands slid up her body and cupped her breasts. "I want to take you right here in front of the world, but we have reservations in an hour."

Turning in his arms, she slid her hands up his chest until they were around his neck and up in his hair. Della pulled his head down and said before she kissed him, "Cancel them."

She felt him growl into her mouth as he returned the kiss, then pulled away from her. "I can't. We're meeting Nathan and Diana."

"Who are they?" she asked and went back to looking out the window. Nathan was from the office, Della was sure.

"Nathan and Diana Andrews from Rodgers. I thought it would be fun to get together with them."

She could tell he was excited to see his old friends. She, on the other hand, had never felt comfortable with people from the office. Della wrapped her arms around her stomach to calm the swarm of anxiety-induced butterflies. Could she face these people for Max? Yes. Would she embarrass herself so badly that he never talked to her again? Most likely.

She felt his arms go around her again, and this time he whispered, "They're going to love you as much as I do. Just be yourself."

Did he just say he loved her? Oh, god. *Hold it together*, she told herself. He didn't mean it that way. This was just a summer fling. Pulling out of his arms, she turned and pushed past him, saying, "I have to get ready then."

Once she got the bathroom door closed behind her, she slid down the door and sat on the floor. It was over; she had to end it now. Love was never supposed to be a part of this. This was a fling, nothing more. She was too much in love with him to let him be in love with her.

The tile floor was cold under her butt and legs, and she had to get up before Max came to see what was wrong. As she shed the business outfit she'd worn during the day, she lectured herself on how to handle herself in a business setting. She would get through this night, and then she would end this non-relationship with Max.

Della unzipped the teal dress she had packed for supper with Max and Max alone. How was it going to look to his friends? Della inwardly groaned—it was going to look desperate. All she had was the jeans and black tank top she was going to wear home tomorrow. Nothing in between.

Pulling out her phone, she sent a text to Max.

Della: What are you wearing?

Della waited for his response as she sat on the side of the tub, but he didn't send one. Instead, walked into the bathroom with her. Crouching down between her legs, he said huskily, "I want to see you in that dress, Hart."

"Okay," she whispered back. Max grabbed it and handed it to her, then he kissed her on the forehead and walked out of the bathroom.

She sighed and gave one last glance at the teal fabric before getting up and sliding the dress over her head. Pulling the pins holding her hair on top of her head, Della watched her curls fall onto her shoulders, then pushed them back so that they all fell down her back. With her fingers, she fluffed them a little, but they looked good anyway. She slid her bag to the wall and grabbed her shoes before looking in the mirror again. No makeup today. Since she usually didn't wear it, she hadn't packed any.

Della nodded to her reflection in the mirror, then opened the door and almost ran into Max, who had been waiting for her. While she was putting her dress on, he had changed into black slacks and a gray button-up shirt. It matched his eyes, and it took Della's breath away. He was gorgeous. She was going out to a fancy dinner with Max Valentine. Her!

With two steps, he was in front of her and had her face in his hands. "I love the dress and can't wait to take it off you."

"You can do it now," she whispered.

He laughed and kissed her, but only lightly. His hands slid from her face to her arms and hands. Max took her shoes from her, then pulled her hand to his mouth and kissed it. Smiling, he drew her into the living room and sat her on the couch. Crouching down in front of her, he picked up her foot and kissed the arch, sliding his fingers over her painted nails. Della smiled, remembering how he'd watched her paint them two days before. Max then picked up her shoe and slid it onto her foot, zipping up the side zipper. He looked up and winked at her, then repeated the performance with the other one.

Once her shoes were on, he stood and held out a hand. Smiling, he pulled her up and kissed her on the mouth. "Let's go."

The restaurant was across the street from Max's apartment building. When they arrived, the Andrews were already at a table. Max's warm hand was on her back as the waiter led them to the table. Was his hand for support or so she wouldn't bolt out of the restaurant? Maybe both.

After sitting down, Max introduced them, even though they all knew each other. "Della, this is Nathan and Diana Andrews. They worked at Rodgers with us. Nathan, Diana, you remember DC Connor Hart, but she goes by Della now."

Shaking both their hands, she didn't really think that they remembered her. She remembered Nathan better; they had worked on a few cases together over the years. Diana was younger, and they had never worked together, but they had both been there when she'd been fired.

"Della's in private practice now. She opened her own firm and hired her first associate today." Max sounded proud of her.

"Congratulations! It must be exciting to work for yourself." Diana looked at her with interest.

"It is exciting, but it's a lot of work. I'm busier now than I ever was at Rodgers," Della admitted. "But with another lawyer in the office, my workload should lighten up a bit."

"Della's looking to hire two more lawyers by the end of the summer," Max injected.

"Maybe just this one. I want to see how that turns out before I get too many people around," Della replied, more to remind Max than to tell the couple on the other side of the table.

"Nathan, ask her how many clients she has?" Max prompted.

Nathan laughed at his friend. "How many clients do you have, Della?"

"Clients or cases?" she said, thinking, "I have around two hundred clients, but only about one hundred twenty-five cases open right now. Usually, I do get a dozen or more a week."

"Wow," Diana said, eyes going wide. "I have fifteen and thought I was overworked."

Just then, the waiter showed up and asked for their drink orders. As the group glanced at their menus, Della got nervous again. She hated being the one that never drank alcohol; people always wanted to talk about it. But when it was her turn, the waiter didn't ask, just winked and walked off.

Nathan, who was beside her, turned and said, "He didn't take your order, Della."

"That's okay. I'll just drink water for now. I'll get him when he comes back," Della assured the group.

Max looked at her and leaned over. "Are you doing okay?"

With just a nod to answer his question, she knew she would be okay. Turning back to the couple across from her, she asked, "How long have you guys been married?"

Nathan took his wife's hand and said, "Thirteen years."

Looking from one to the other, she replied, "Really! I didn't even know you were married when I was at Rodgers. Any kids?"

The couple looked at each other, and Diana said, "No time for kids. We both work too many hours right now."

Max looked at her in surprise. "You didn't know they were married?"

Della shook her head at him. "No, I told you I didn't listen to gossip in the office. I was there to work, not socialize."

Diana laughed. "I wish I could tune out the office gossip."

When the drinks arrived, the waiter placed one in front of Della. She knew without tasting that the dark drink in the glass in front of her was non-alcoholic but in the same glass as Diana's mixed drink. To her surprise, the waiter also dropped off a small bowl of cherry tomatoes. She smiled at him and said, "Thanks."

Max turned to Nathan and Diana. "Della's law office is in an old mansion. It even has a ballroom."

"It's a small ballroom." Della rolled her eyes at Max.

"It's all oak and has this gorgeous trim. She gets to live upstairs also." Max grinned.

"Do you own it?" Diana asked in awe.

"Yes, it's been in my family for a few generations. It was just sitting empty, so I fixed it up. Well, my carpenter fixed it up," Della admitted with a nod.

"You know, if you two are looking to get out of corporate law, Della's going to need for more lawyers at her firm. She's going to run for judge this fall," Max announced casually, leaning back in his seat.

"I don't know if I'm running or not. I haven't decided." Della said quickly, then threw a glance at Max.

Nathan leaned forward and nodded. "You should run. You would be great. I always went to you when I had big questions; everyone did. I can see you as a judge."

"I don't know." Della wasn't able to convince herself not to run yet.

When the orders came, Della's chicken special had turned into a fish dish. Everyone at the table noticed, but Della just thanked the waiter and started to eat. It was amazing. She knew that Mady had probably made her meal and was happy for her young friend that she had met at the farmer's market years before. Mady had brought her many meals over the years to try, and Della recognized her food right away.

Nathan looked at her meal and frowned. "Della, that's not what you ordered."

Looking up, she said, "I don't remember what I ordered. This is really good, though."

Max turned to her. "You can't let people run over you like that. I'm going to return the dish."

"No, you're not," Della argued.

"Della."

"*Max.*"

Della turned back to her plate and started to eat the food. When the waiter came by to ask how everything tasted, Della asked, "Very good. Is the chef a woman?"

The waiter smiled at her. "Yes, and she would like to treat your table to dessert."

"No, we'll be okay," Della replied.

"She insists. Is chocolate okay with everyone?" The waiter asked the table but didn't actually look at anyone but Della.

The three others agreed with the dessert selection except Della. "No chocolate for me, Josh."

With his questions answered, the waiter left them alone again. Looking up from her meal, she noticed all eyes were on her.

Nathan asked, "Do you know him? You know his name."

"He said his name when he first came to the table. I've never met him before." Della shrugged.

Max raised an eyebrow at her but let her steer the conversation to everyone else's meal choices. Once everyone was done, the waiter came by and cleared off the table. Once the last of the dishes was taken away, a waitress came out with the dessert tray. Everyone got a slice of chocolate cake, but Della received layered cake filled with strawberries.

Della let out an excited laugh and jumped from the table to hug the waitress. "You must be the chef tonight!"

"I am, for almost a year now," the chef said.

Turning to the table, Della introduced her. "Madalyn Nelson, this is Nathan and Diana Andrews, and this is Max Valentine."

As she shook hands around the table, Mady said to the group, "Della got me through summer school algebra, trigonometry, and Shakespeare. Without her, I would still be in high school."

Mady looked back at Della. "How are Evie and Ben? Dad says she got married."

"I couldn't believe it either. Ben is twelve and taller than me. My other sister started to work with her," Della replied, forgetting the rest of the group.

"Dad said so as well. She's a redhead too, but then again, so are you." Mady laughed at Della.

Della touched her hair. "How's Jacob? Are you still together?"

Mady smiled and lifted her hand. "We're engaged."

Della grabbed her hand, looking at the sparkling ring and said, "Now you have to name your first born after me."

"Don't worry, Jacob's already approved that." Mady laughed again.

"Did she introduce you guys?" Diana asked eagerly.

Mady beamed at her. "No, but she told me how to get his attention."

"How?" Diana asked.

"It's a secret, but he loves tomatoes now," Mady told the table, playfully bumping her shoulder into Della's.

"It was just an idea at the time, but since it worked for you so many years ago, I tried it this summer. I think it turned out okay," Della told her, and Mady looked over at Max and winked.

"I have to get back to work. It was great to see you, Della." Mady hugged her again.

"Mady, you have to call me when you have time. There's a lot of stuff we need to catch up on," Della said as the younger woman walked away.

Sitting down again, she picked up her fork and noticed that everyone was staring at her. Blushing, she put her fork down to explain. "Mady's parents run the stand next to Evie's, and I tutored her during the day. We became close friends. This is one of the dishes she used to make me as payment for helping her. It was my favorite."

Max leaned back. "Did you know she was the chef here?"

"No. Last I heard, she was studying in Paris, but I really haven't talked to her parents this year, and last year, I didn't help much at the stand. Zoey had taken over," she explained.

"When did you know she was the Chef?" he asked.

"When I got the fish. I know this dish, I used to eat it twice a month for six months straight. I know Mady's fish recipe." Della grinned. "I had my suspicions when I got a drink and a side of tomatoes without being asked."

"So, you worked at a farmer's market?" Nathan asked.

"Yep. Every Saturday with my sister. She had nobody else to help, so I helped as much as I could," Della answered.

Diana looked at her curiously. "Is that why you never went on the retreats?"

"No, I really didn't want to go on those. It was just a party, and I gave up partying a long time ago." Della caught Max just staring at her.

Turning to her uneaten dessert, she hoped the conversation would move away from her. Taking a bite of the cake, she knew her friend had also made this. Della looked back up and noticed Max was still staring at her while the other couple were eating their dessert in silence. She knew she had messed up, she shouldn't have talked to Mady so much, but it was nice to see a friendly face.

The table was still silent when the waiter came with the bill. Placing one between each couple. Della grabbed at it, but Max was too fast and pulled out his credit card and put it in the folder.

Max started the conversation again, breaking the silence. "You guys should think about leaving Rodgers. I bet Della would hire you."

Della almost choked on her dessert. "Max."

"I don't know. It sounds interesting. More laid back, fewer hours. More time for life," Nathan said.

"Drive out to Birch Cove one day, and we can poke around and see if you would like small-town life. Della will need some experienced lawyers when she becomes a judge," Max replied, laying his hand on her thigh.

"I don't know about being a judge, but I would like some experience. I do hope Max didn't just set this meal up to get you guys to leave your jobs. I would still be at Rodgers if I could."

Diana looked at Nathan, who shook his head, then Diana turned away from him and said, "Grant got fired last month. He was stealing work from another lawyer, and he had been banging his secretary for years. His wife left him, and her father sacked him."

Della sat up. "Really? He deserved it all."

Nathan laughed at her response. "Yes, he did."

When the waiter had run the credit cards, he brought a bag for Della. "From the chef," he said. With a smile, she thanked him, asking him to thank Mady as well. Both couples got up and were saying goodbye by the door when Diana gave her a quick hug and whispered, "You're great for Max."

Max and Della held hands as they walked across the road back to his apartment building. They got into the empty elevator, and he backed her into a corner and lowered his lips to her neck, then kissed his way over to her shoulder. "What's in the bag?"

"I don't know," she answered, enjoying the feel of his lips on her skin.

"Open it."

Pulling away from her, he took the bag in his hands and held it for her. Inside the bag was just over a dozen cherry tomatoes. "That's what I figured. Mady thought up the tomato trick a few summers ago."

Max carried the bag for her as the elevator stopped on his floor, then took her hand and walked her to the door. Stopping, he handed the bag back to her and unlocked the door. Once they were inside, he pulled her into the apartment and wrapped her in his arms. "Now I can finally peel that dress off you."

Smiling up at him, she couldn't help but melt in his arms. Would she ever get used to the fact that she got to sleep with Max Valentine? His lips brushed hers lightly as his hands ran up her back and into her long curls. The kiss deepened as Della felt his tongue dip into her mouth, and with a moan, she met his tongue with her own. She dropped the bag on the floor and slid her hand up his chest, pulling his shirt from his pants as she went.

Dragging his lips from hers, he lifted her into his arms and carried her to the bedroom. Max set her gently on the edge of the bed and crouched down in front of her, then picked up her foot and slowly slid the shoe off. He grabbed her bare foot in his hand and started kissing each of her toes, then ran his tongue up her instep and gently bit her heel. He then took the other foot and did the same thing.

Della watched him loving her feet and then gasped as he moved up her legs, pushing up her dress as he went. Her breath caught as he pulled down her panties and threw them over his shoulder. Returning his attention to her, she watched him slide his hand over her core, making her shudder from the pleasure.

Slowly and lightly, his fingers slipped into her folds, finding her most sensitive spot. Unable to hold herself up with her arms, she fell back onto the bed as his mouth replace the fingers, bringing her over the edge almost instantly. With her body still feeling the echoes of her climax, she watched Max stand up and start removing his clothes. His eyes were on her as he started to undo his shirt, starting with the cuffs, then the rest, but after only two buttons, he grabbed at it and pulled.

Della laughed as buttons flew across the room, and he shrugged out of the torn shirt.

Grabbing his fly, she sat up and shoved his hands away, undoing his pants for him. Leaning forward, she stared into his eyes as she placed a gentle kiss just above the button. Slowly Della slid the zipper down and slipped her hand into the opening, gently caressing his penis as it twitched in her hand. Della bit her lip, then moved her hands to his hips and slid his pants and briefs down his legs.

As he kicked the pants away, she ran her hands back up his thighs until they held on to his backside. Locking eyes with him again, she leaned forward and slowly took him into her mouth. Max gasped at the move. Taking her time, she caressed him with her mouth, then picked up the pace as he moaned her name and shoved his fingers in her hair.

She'd felt him tightening below his shaft and knew he was close. Suddenly, he pushed her down on to the bed, but instead of joining her, Max flipped her onto her stomach and lifted her butt to him. He yanked up her dress and entered her fast, growling into her ear as his testicles slammed into her core. Meeting his thrusts with her own, she moaned his name as she came, feeling him come within moments of her.

Slowly, he pulled out of her and gathered her into his arms as he climbed onto the bed. His body was hot behind her, and the dress, while comfortable to wear, was not comfortable to lay in. Sitting up, she tugged the dress over her head and tossed it on the floor. Della looked down at Max. His eyes were closed, and he was smiling. He was absolutely beautiful, and for today, Max Valentine was hers.

CHAPTER 16

MAX WOKE up as the sun came up over the city on the other side of the window. The bed was empty, and Della was gone. Putting on some shorts, he walked out to the living room to see she was on the couch. He could tell she was watching the sunrise over the city. She was fully dressed, and her hair up in a loose bun at her nape.

He kissed the top of her head as he leaned over her from behind the couch. "Morning, beautiful."

"Good morning, Max Valentine," she said.

Looking down at her, he thought her voice was shaky as she spoke. She had a few files spread out on the couch, but her computer was closed. Had she been working or just watching the city below?

"Do you want to come back to bed, Hart?" he asked. He really liked calling her by her last name. He had noticed over the weeks that her sisters' husbands called them by their maiden name as a term of endearment.

"No, I have to get back. I have work to do." She didn't sound very convincing.

"Looks like you got some work done already today," he observed.

"Not much, but I did file the paperwork to get on the ballot in November," she replied but didn't smile or look at him.

Max walked around the couch and gathered up some folders. Putting them on the coffee table, he sat down and pulled her into his arms. "Congratulations, sweetheart."

"I'm more scared than happy at this point. I have a lot to do in a few months." Della sighed in his arms.

"Well, it's time to get happy, Della. We're going out to celebrate." He kissed the top of her head again.

"It's six in the morning, Max."

"And we have the city at our feet. I think we can find a great breakfast place." He hugged her tight and let her go.

As the water washed over him a few minutes later, he hoped she would join him in the shower. The thought consumed him until he turned off the water, and she hadn't entered the bathroom. He couldn't shake the feeling something was happening with her.

Last night he was sure he had made a mistake making her go to supper with Nathan and Diana, but within minutes, she was holding her own and was the Della he knew. Even when the conversation had turned to Grant, she hadn't let it bother her. He had been worried when she wouldn't stand up for herself, wondering if she was falling back into letting everyone roll over her. Then her friend had come out, and she had explained what had actually been happening. He'd seen the Della he loved come out in public.

Once her friend had left the table, she had gotten quiet again, and Max didn't understand why. Since then, even though they had made love when they'd gotten back to the apartment, she hadn't perked up. They had the entire day in front of them in Minneapolis, and he hoped he could get her back to herself.

Walking out of the bathroom, he saw Della sitting on the bed, typing into her phone. Today she was in jeans and loose black tank top with a gray sweater over the top. She wore the same sandals from the night before, and seeing them made the blood rush to his groin.

She looked up at him, no smile on her face or in her green eyes. "I have to get back. One of my clients has been hospitalized."

"What happened?" he asked, grabbing pants from the brawer.

"She took out a restraining order on her husband. He didn't like it." She got up and walked out of the room.

Watching her walk out the door, he knew he had lost his day with Della. By the time he pulled into the driveway at the mansion, he knew she was heading to the hospital in her car. There had been half a dozen phone calls that she had taken since they had made it out of the city. She had called her client's doctor, her client's mother, Lea to go over details of the job, Casey to see when he could start, Evie, and Zoey. When she exited his car without a goodbye, she was on the phone with Gabe, the arresting officer.

Chad was painting when they had pulled up, and Max saw he was almost done. In another month, he would be done, then what would Della have him do? In the past month, he had noticed she liked having the young man around and liked that she was able to make sure he had money. That's how she was. Even her new hires were somewhat adrift, and she had thrown them a lifeline.

Max waved at Chad and took Della's bag into the house. He had no need for a bag since they had stayed at his apartment. As he walked up the stairs, he realized he hadn't felt at home when he was in the city. But walking into this house felt right. When they'd left for the trip, he had taken a box of books he no longer needed to his apartment, but he hadn't taken anything back to Birch Cove.

In mid-afternoon, he went across the street for a snack with the aunts. He loved spending time with them. Now that he knew that they weren't sisters, he loved listening to them talk about the young people around them. He watched for signs of affection. There weren't many, but he'd caught something every once in a while.

"How was your trip?" Mae asked.

"Good. Della hired two people. A lawyer, and an office manager."

"She needed help," Sally said, nodding.

"How was the trip for you two?" Sally asked and winked at him.

"It was great, but you knew it would be, Sally," he said back to her.

"Mae thought it would all go south. Hart girls have a hard time with happiness."

Max looked at the woman and wondered if she was right. Was Della's sadness yesterday and this morning due to her being happy? Was she happy and not happy about it? He had learned that both her sisters had bad breakups before they got together with their husbands.

Choosing another cookie, Max realized that he wanted to be Della's husband. He wanted her for life. It had been weeks since he'd thought of a life without her.

"I hope you're wrong, Mae. I think she's my Hart."

Sally squealed and laughed. Mae looked down her nose at him and said, "You will have to make sure she wants to give you hers. Della's not your typical girl, Max."

"I know." He grabbed another cookie and left. He had a few things to do before Della made it home for the night. Bounding up the stairs in his rush, he almost tripped over Della sitting in the corner at the top of the stairs. She had been sitting with her back against the corner, her arms wrapped around her legs and chin resting on her knees.

"What's wrong?" he asked, sinking to the floor in front of her.

She didn't turn to him, just stared ahead of her. "Beth died. I couldn't save her."

Max's heart broke for her. She was taking responsibility for this woman's death. Another lost soul she had tried to save, but this time was unable to.

"Della, it's not your fault. It's her husband's. You did everything you could," he assured her.

"I should have sent her to Minneapolis. When a case is bad, I send them down there. I know a few lawyers who will help them get residency in another county and file down there. I should've sent her away. I didn't think it would end like this," she said as the tears ran down her face.

"How many have you sent to Minneapolis?" He had never heard her talk about this. She was always confident that she would win for these women.

"A few. One too short," she whispered.

"Della, you did everything you could have. You can never predict what will happen," Max replied, sliding closer to her on the floor.

"Her girls are three and four, and they'll never know why their mom left them. I was twelve, and I don't know why mine left me. Their grandma doesn't know if she can take care of them. What's going to happen to them, Max?" The tears were still coming.

"It'll be okay. They'll be fine," he soothed, touching her foot.

"No, Max, it'll never be okay for them again." He barely heard her whisper.

"You had your dad," Max said as he gathered her into his arms.

"No, I never had my dad. He was there, but he was never there for me. His job was to raise me, not to be there when I needed him. I only spoke to him once after I turned sixteen about anything other than Evie and Zoey. I didn't come when Evie called to say he was dying. We had nothing to say to each other in life, so we had nothing to say in death." Her tears had stopped.

Max looked at her. "I wish you'd had a better relationship with him."

"My life would have been very different if my mother had taken me when she'd left. Probably for the best." She wiped the remaining tears off her face.

"If you hadn't had the life you've had, Della Hart, I would've never fallen in love with you." As he said the words, he felt her stiffen in his arms.

"You don't love me, Max. This was just a fling. When you go back to Minneapolis, you'll realize that." She pulled away from him completely as she spoke.

"No, Della, I want to stay here with you."

Getting up, he followed her into the bedroom, knowing he would have a hard time convincing her of his feelings. The woman was unable to take a complement, so how was she going to react to feelings?

"You, Max Valentine? You want to stay in this dinky town? Soon you'll miss the parties and your friends. This is no life for you," she said, then added, "This was only a fling, until your book was done."

"My book has been done for almost a week," he said quietly.

"Then this is over. Get your stuff together and get out," she replied, biting her lower lip.

"Della, the fling was over a long time ago. It turned into a relationship." He took a step towards her but stopped when she took a step back.

Della shook her head. "I don't do relationships, Max. That's not me."

"Liar."

"I am not."

"I am in love with you, and I want to marry you, Della Hart," he insisted, laying his feelings bare.

"You deserve better than me. I'm just a few nice nights between the sheets, not the forever kind," she bit out and grabbed his suitcase, then opened the drawers he kept his stuff in.

"Maybe if you would give it a chance, you would see that forever would be great." He had no idea what she was talking about, couldn't she see it?

"You understood before we slept together that this was just a fling, Max. I cannot give you more than that." Her voice waivered, but she kept filling the suitcase with his clothes.

"What the hell are you talking about? Why are you so undeserving of happiness?" he yelled.

"This is not going to work, Max, you knew it all along. I don't fit into your world, and you don't fit into mine." She closed the bag.

"If we tried ..." he said quietly.

"We wouldn't succeed, Max. You need to find someone who fits into your world and get married and have kids." As she handed him his bag, her eyes were cast down at the floor between them.

"I want to marry you, and have kids with you, Della," he pleaded.

"I am not having kids, Max. I want you to have kids. I want to see little Max Valentines one day."

"Is there anything I can say that will get through that thick head of yours?" His eyes met her green ones. He could see tears filling them.

"No. I'm going for a walk, and when I get back, I want you gone." She walked past him and out of the room, then he heard her walking down the stairs.

Standing in the middle of the room with his bag, he wondered what had went so wrong. He was going to ask her to marry him, and he had, but she had ended it instead. She had ripped out his heart and stomped it into the ground.

He gathered all his things, and after four trips to the car, he took one last look around at Della's world, the one he had been kicked out of. It hadn't taken him long to remove any trace that he'd been there. Maybe his heart would heal as fast as that, but he didn't think so.

CHAPTER 17

THE FRONT DOOR slammed again for the fourth time. Was it the last time? Maybe he would come in again. Della listened to his every move as he'd packed. When she had made it to the bottom of the stairs, she had been unable to leave the house, and her legs had started giving out on her. Slipping into the ballroom, she slid to the floor in a corner of the dark, empty room.

From there, she had listened to him moving throughout the house, gathering his things, removing himself from her life. With each step he took, more tears flowed from her eyes. By the fourth slam of the door, her sobs were echoing off the walls around her.

Max Valentine had said he loved her and wanted to marry her. Her, Della Connor Hart. The words were her every fantasy come true. How many times had she watched him at the office, wanting him to just notice her? Now he loved her, but there was no way he could love her as much as she has loved him for so long.

She had let them get too deep. She should've sent him away weeks ago, but she was enjoying being with Max too much and couldn't do it. Now she had let it go too long, and she had hurt him. Hurting him had almost killed her. The pain in his eyes was going to haunt her forever.

Her heart was breaking, and Della curled up on the floor in a ball, hoping it would ease the pain. It didn't. She knew the pain would be worse when he realized he wanted kids and she couldn't give them to him. He would leave her then, after a few months or maybe even a couple of years. Either way, she would be devastated. Maybe she should've waited. At least he wouldn't have been hurt then. She would've taken the pain for both of them.

Lying on the floor, her mind drifted to Max and his future. He would find a tall, beautiful blonde and fall in love with her. Then they would have two kids, and they would look like Max and be adorable. He would be happy with her, maybe he would bring them to visit his aunts, and Della would be able to get a glimpse of him and his life.

A fresh wave of tears obscured her vision of the empty ballroom. Sobs racked her body as she let herself dream of being able to carry Max's baby. She wanted his baby more than anything she had ever wanted in her life. Why was her life so unfair that she could never have the man or family she wanted? Happiness just wasn't in the cards for her.

Della didn't know how long she'd laid on the floor of the empty ballroom, but when she'd finally forced herself up, the room was in complete darkness. The only light was moonlight coming in through the windows. She only made it a few feet when she slid down the wall again, but was able to sit up right. At least for now

Knowing she had until morning to get it together, she let herself just sit against the wall. The tears were now gone, but the pain was still just as strong.

Della suddenly heard a loud pounding on the door, but she ignored it. There was nobody she wanted to see right now. Her hope that the person would leave was dashed when she heard the door open, then she heard Evie's voice yelling through the house. Della tried to call to her sister, but nothing came out of her mouth.

Listening to her sister run through the house, yelling her name, Della tried to get to her feet. This time she could only sit—her legs wouldn't move her. When the ballroom door slammed open, Evie saw her in the square of light the open door cast across the room.

"Shut the door, Evie," Della whispered at her sister.

Evie did, and Della heard her walking through the dark towards her. Evie sat down with a sigh, and both sisters were silent for a long time. Evie's phone rang and lit up the room. She looked at the screen, then answered it. "Zoey, we're in the ballroom." Then she hung it up, and the room went dark again.

Silently, they sat until Zoey showed up, and she sat down on the other side of Della. Each sister took one of Della's hands in theirs.

Zoey was the first to speak. "Is he gone?"

"Yes," Della whispered.

"Was he a jerk?" Evie asked.

"No, I was," Della admitted.

"What was wrong with him?" Zoey asked.

"Nothing, he's Max Valentine," Della said, still loving to say his name out loud.

Evie raised an eyebrow. "Then what's wrong with you?"

Della bit her lip as a lump formed in her throat. "I'm broken."

"You're not broken, Della. You're the strongest one of us all. I didn't know that until last year, but you did things I never could have." Evie squeezed her hand in the dark.

Della was silent as she thought about Evie's words. Was she really the strongest of them all? They sat silent again for a long time. "You guys are stronger than me. Evie, you raised Ben all by yourself and farmed for years without anyone to help, and Zoey fought in a war."

"I was able to raise my son. It was a gift I never knew I was given. I know I've complained about it, but now I know that it was an honor. Farming came naturally to me. I don't know what else I would have done," Evie admitted.

"I just did what I was told. That's what it is like to be a soldier, Della," Zoey said.

"No, you did more, and you did it by yourself. We weren't there enough for you. Ever," Della said, shaking her head.

"You guys had other things going on; you had lives," Zoey said, then sniffed in the darkness.

Della looked over at Zoey. "I should've been there when you got off the plane in Minneapolis, but I worked instead. I should have been there for you. Something was bothering you when you came back, and I never even asked you about it. I should've asked you."

"Gabe helped me through it, and I wouldn't have talked to you about it anyway. I'm a Hart; we tend to not talk about things," Zoey replied.

"Maybe one day, you'll talk to us." Della squeezed her hand.

The room went silent as the sisters thought about the past. Zoey's voice was small when she said into the darkness. "I was raped in Afghanistan."

Both sister's gasped and pulled Zoey into a hug. "I never knew," Evie said.

"I wish you would have told me," Della's voice cracked.

"Gabe helped; he saw right away that something was wrong. Having been through war, he knew I was having a hard time. He was great and helped me through the night terrors. I wasn't sleeping at all in the beginning."

"I wish I would have known. I was mean to him at first," Evie said.

"You were, but you came through in the end and got us back together." Zoey hugged Evie, but Della was sandwiched between them.

Evie laughed and replied, "Confession time, is it? Greg and I never had sex. Ben isn't his son."

"What?" Zoey said loudly. "Does he know?"

"Ben?" Evie asked.

"Yes, Ben. I assume Greg knew, and Jasper, does he know?" Zoey asked.

"No, Ben doesn't know yet. I'm waiting for him to grow up a bit more. Yes, Jasper knows. I told him before I slept with him the second time."

Della looked at her sister in the dim light. "The second time?"

"The first was kind of an accident, but it gave us Willow. I actually got pregnant the first two times I had sex. Can anyone top that?" Evie laughed at herself.

Zoey sat up and asked, "So you and Greg never …?"

Evie looked at her sisters, "Greg was gay. He had no interest in me as anything but a cover."

"Wow," Zoey said.

Silence engulfed the room again as the memories surrounded the women in the darkness. Della knew it was her turn, but she liked everything buried and wasn't ready to bring it up.

"Any confessions, Della?" Zoey asked.

"Nope, my life is known to all." Della lied.

"Why'd you break it off with Max?" Evie looked at her. Della had thought she would bring up her secret.

"He had the nerve to fall in love with me and wanted to marry me." She tried to joke about it.

"How dare he!" Zoey said and laughed.

Evie took her hand again and added, "But you love him, and I think you would like to marry him."

"We have different futures," Della replied. Tears were threatening again.

"Love, marriage, and kids. Which of those don't you want, Della?" Evie asked.

"It's not what I want. It's what I can't have, Evie," Della said.

"Just because you couldn't have the first one doesn't mean you cannot have more." Evie looked at her intently. Della wanted to hug her sister for her cryptic speech. Evie was letting Della be the one to bring it up to Zoey.

"Yes, it does. I can't have any more; it's one and done for me," Della whispered.

"Are you sure? Have you talked to anyone?" Evie demanded, wanting to fix everything for her older sister.

"I don't need to, Evie. Within an hour of her birth, I hemorrhaged. They did a complete hysterectomy that day. Some girls get cars for their sixteenth birthday, but not me. I got everything taken away." Della leaned her head back against the wall.

Zoey looked at the two having a conversation she didn't understand. "What are you talking about?"

"I got pregnant in college, and our father forced me to put her up for adoption. Evie found out last fall, but I didn't tell her that the baby was big, over nine pounds, and I had her naturally. I was able to hold her for a few minutes before I passed out. When I came to, the baby was gone, and I was never going to have another one," Della admitted to her youngest sister.

"You were sixteen?" Zoey asked.

"She was born on my birthday. I was alone, and Dad came the next day. He couldn't be bothered."

"He was probably busy, Della." Evie defended.

"I was in the hospital for days Evie. He only came the day I had to sign the papers. He didn't even come when I was discharged," Della said.

"I still don't believe he'd do that."

"I do. I see him doing that to you. That's the dad I got too." Zoey pulled Della into her arms.

"Evie got lucky with her dad. We didn't." Della looked at Zoey.

"Have you ever met her? Was she a red head?" Zoey asked.

"I saw her once and have a picture that they took in the nursery. She had dark hair, like Willow, but actually darker. I sent a letter a few weeks ago. She turns eighteen this year. Maybe I'll hear from her," Della said softly.

"Is that why you don't hold the babies?" Zoey asked.

"It's better not to know how it feels, than long for what can never be." Della shrugged.

Zoey squeezed Della's hand. "So, what did you break up with Max for?"

"I want him to have kids of his own. He deserves that," Della answers.

"So, you cast him aside for his own good so that he could possibly have kids of his own?" Evie asked.

Della sighed. "He would start to resent me for not being able to give him what he wants."

"Does he want kids?" Zoey asked.

"Everybody wants kids."

Zoey shrugged. "Gabe didn't, but I made him."

"Maybe you should ask him," Evie said.

Della scrunched her knees in tighter to her chest. "No, we shouldn't have been together anyway."

"Why not?" Zoey asked.

Della chuckled. "Because he's Max Valentine, Zoey."

"You say his name like he is an actor or something."

"I worked with him for ten years, and he never noticed me. I was nothing to him. He was that guy who had it all: the girls loved him, and the guys wanted to be his friend. I loved him then too, from afar," Della explained.

"You have him! He's so into you, he can't take his eyes off you when you're in the room." Zoey rolled her eyes at Della.

"That's only because there's nobody in this town, so he just turned his attention to me while he was here. At first, I kept away from him. He was suddenly interested in me. *Me.* Then I decided to just let it happen and see how far it would go. I had Max Valentine in my bed. Me!"

"You deserve Max Valentine in your bed." Evie nudged her foot into Della's.

"He belongs in the city. It was just a small-town fling, and he'll get over me in no time."

"And you?" Zoey asked.

Della was quiet for a moment before answering, "I'll never get over him." Her words echoed off the walls as the room went silent.

"What are you going to do?" Evie asked.

Della shrugged, defeated. "Tomorrow I go back to work. I have two employees coming soon, and tomorrow I start campaigning for Judge."

"You're doing it?" Zoey asked.

Della nodded. "I filed this morning. My name will be on the ballot. I just have to get people to vote for me."

"You have my vote. Max isn't the only one who thinks you'll be a great judge." Evie smiled.

By the time her sisters left her house, the sun was starting to come up. They had spent time going over what was needed to be done to get her campaign off the ground. The night had ended with them all promising that there would be no secrets anymore among them. Each had taken a few bricks out of the walls that had put up between them.

Della felt better than she'd thought she would. As she got ready for the day, she realized that her heart was still broken, but maybe she would be able to live with the pain. Just living was all she could focus on now.

CHAPTER 18

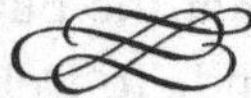

The ballroom was bright and sunny as the afternoon light shown in the windows. It was finally the first Tuesday in November: election day. Della had worked towards this day for months. As she stood there, people all over the county were voting for her. Or not.

Looking around, she was happy to see all her loved ones milling about the room, eating snacks, and talking. Both her sisters and their spouses were there, babies in tow. Ben and Jasper's cousin Clem were playing video games on handheld devices in the corner. She would have to keep an eye on those two in the next few years.

Jasper's grandma was talking to Casey and Lea by the punch. Both had arrived in August, and by October, they'd moved in together. It had surprised Della. She hadn't noticed anything was happening. Lea had laughed at her boss, saying Della noticed very little that went on around her.

Both Lea and Casey had been perfectly suited for her office. Casey had picked up the routine and knew what was expected of him within a week. He seemed to enjoy not working in security. He'd also come in handy when a husband had shown up to take his wife home. Neither of the women knew what to do, but Casey took over the situation. That might've been when the couple moved in together—Della wasn't exactly sure.

Lea had been the type of lawyer that wouldn't be pushed around. The judges had been unable to intimidate her. Her personality was completely different from Della's, but the two of them had become friends. Lea even came over to watch movies with Della on Saturday afternoons. Sometimes she would bring her girls with her.

Lea and Casey were joined at the punch bowl by Diana Andrews, followed closely by her husband. To Della's utter surprise, the couple had shown up at her door a few weeks after their dinner together, and she showed them around town and around the office. They had both been eager to join her firm. She now had three great lawyers in her office. They all got along, and the office was a lively place. Very different from Rodgers and associates.

Moving past the chatting couples, she spotted Sally and Mae talking to another neighbor at one of the tables that had been brought over to the party. They were still doing great, even though Chad had finished the kitchen last week and had moved on to fixing up Nathan and Diana's house down the block. It was too far for Sally to see him every day, but some days he would stop by to say hi.

The only one missing was Max, but she hadn't heard from him since he'd left. Nathan had told her he was doing okay. She tried not to think about him and what could've been. He was better off without her.

As her mind had drifted to Max, she had missed hearing the thumping feet running though the ballroom until she was hit by a little body. Stooping down, she pulled the little girl into her arms. "Molly, you can't run in the house, baby." But her voice was not scolding has she pulled the three-year-old into a hug.

The little brown-haired girl hugged her back and said, "But I missed you so much, Mommy Della." Della's heart melted, and she hugged the little girl again.

After Beth's death, her mother decided she couldn't raise her daughter's children. She wasn't healthy enough to raise a three- and four-year-old. Della hadn't hesitated to adopt the little girls. Within a month, they had moved in, and it had been a difficult time. She had two new employees and two new kids, and it had kept her mind off Max during most days, but the memories would wrap around her at night.

Over Molly's head, she saw Lily walking into the room, holding Nora's hand. Lily was wearing a blue dress that matched Molly's, and both had their long brown hair in a braid. Nora was her nanny, and Della waved at the young woman, who started her way into the room.

"She got away from me, Della," Nora explained. Molly always got away from her.

"It's maybe too big of a day for naps, Nora, but thanks for your help. You can go for the day, and we'll see you tomorrow," Della said and slid the smaller of the two girls down to the floor. Taking each of their hands in hers she went to mingle with her family and friends.

It was still hours before the final votes would be cast and counted, but by then, all these people would be home and in bed. They were here now, and she planned to enjoy it while it lasted.

She would swing by Mae and Sally's table first since they were sure to be the first to leave today. They had to get home for supper, and once they were gone, the group would order pizza.

She couldn't stop smiling as she watched the two little girls fight to crawl onto Sally's lap. They had loved her the moment they'd met her, and Sally had instantly loved them back. "Molly and Lily! How are you two doing?" Sally asked them.

They giggled at her and started jabbering at the older woman. Della turned to Mae, who usually had a comment about the two little girls. When she saw the older woman's face, her smile disappeared.

"Mae, are you okay?" Della said, grabbing her hand. "Mae?"

The woman didn't respond back to her, just sat stone-faced. Her eyes suddenly rolled back in their sockets as Della watched. Della gasped and yelled to the room, "Somebody call an ambulance!"

The next few minutes were gone in a second, but they felt like hours. When the ambulance finally showed up, all the kids had been hustled upstairs, and Della was holding Sally in her arms as the older woman cried. Zoey said she would take the girls home with her while Della drove Sally to the hospital.

As they drove, Sally asked her to call Mae's niece, Elizabeth. So,

Della called Max's mom. It was the first time she had ever talked to the woman who'd raised the man she loved.

When they got to the hospital, Sally went to sit with Mae, who was covered in tubes and surrounded by machines. Della went out to sit in the waiting room to wait.

CHAPTER 19

MAX HAD BEEN SCANNING the internet for election results for local elections. He hadn't found anything when his mother had called him, saying something had happened to Mae, and that she was heading to Birch Cove to see her. Max had insisted he would drive.

After picking up his mother, they had spent the drive talking about Mae and Sally. Max found out that they had met in college, and when Mae's mother got sick, both women came home to take care of her. They had never been apart since then. His mother told stories that made him laugh, and he shared stories from the previous summer, from Sally's crushes to their constant bickering.

Though he talked a lot, he didn't say anything about Della. When he had returned from Birch Cove, he told his mom about her but hadn't brought her up since. Maybe his mother thought that he was already over her, but instead, he just found it too painful to talk about her.

Did his mother know how much he loved the stubborn woman? He didn't know. Did he still love that stubborn woman? Yes, with every breath he took.

When Nathan and Diana had told him they were going to work for Della, he was happy for them. The couple had been having trouble, and a more laid-back life was what they needed, but he had told them that day that he didn't want to hear anything about her. At that time, he'd still been angry with the redhead. Was he still angry? Yes, but not as much.

The two-hour drive had taken him just under one and a half. Max dropped his mother off at the door before parking the car, and he climbed out into the chilly air. Looking up at the hospital, he wondered if he would see Della today? Tomorrow? Maybe she wouldn't even come.

Was he ready to face her again? It had been four months since he'd held her in his arms, and they still ached to hold her. Would it always be like this?

At the desk, he asked for Mae's room and was told the family was meeting in a waiting room. The nurse's face didn't give anything away, but he knew that was bad. As he got closer, he could see a doctor talking to his mother, who was holding Sally in her arms. When the entire room came into view, he stopped and stared. Della was seated in a chair behind them, wearing a dark blue dress, and her hair was piled on her head in some kind of hairstyle that looked stunning on her. She looked better than the night she wore the teal dress if that was possible.

Silently taking a chair next to Della, he listened to the doctor describe a stroke. Though everyone had tried to save her, it was too late. She was already gone. When the doctor was quiet, Sally asked, "Can I see her one more time?"

"Yes," the doctor replied softly.

"I'll take you," his mother said. The two women followed the doctor down the hallway, leaving Della and Max alone in the room.

Della was staring at a tissue clenched in her hand. "She was at my house when it happened. We were having a party for the election."

"It's not your fault, Della," Max said. He wanted to touch her but couldn't bear it.

"I know. But I feel bad just the same."

"You always take the world on your shoulders." He leaned back in the chair. "What are you going to do with Sally?" Della asked. "She has no family that I know of."

"I don't think I have to make that decision today," Max answered on a sigh. He rubbed his hands over his face.

"You're inheriting the house," Della commented quietly.

"Do you know that, or are you guessing?" Maybe he'd said that a little too harshly, based on her flinch.

Della peeked up at him. "I wrote the will."

"I'll just let Sally live there then."

"Sally can't live alone; she has spells. Mae was having a hard time with her lately," she explained.

"Well, I'll have to move her in with me then, and we'll sell the place. I don't want it anyway." He got up to look out the window. The sun was starting to set in the distance.

"Don't sell it, Max. It's your inheritance," she whispered. Max wondered why she even cared.

"Why did she leave it to me, and not my mom or sisters? You're her lawyer; you should know why," Max demanded.

Della shrugged. "Because you're Maximillian."

"You mean Max Valentine, as you like to say," he bit back at her.

"You don't understand. Mae's dad was named Maximillian. You were named after him," she said.

Turning from the window, he leaned against the frame and asked, "So my great grandparents were named Maximillian and Delphinea? That's rich. Why did you kick me out, Della?" He had sworn to himself he wouldn't ask, wouldn't bring it up. He was going to get on with his life and forget about this woman.

"No, don't start."

"I deserve to know what I did wrong," he demanded, glaring at her from across the room.

"It wasn't you. It was me. It's always me," Della answered.

Max scoffed. "That's what they all say, Della."

"It was time. I had wasted enough of your time."

"I never said you were a waste of time, Della. I was having the time of my life!"

"Just let it go. I can't go through this again," she said to the window.

"*You* go through it? I'm the one who thought that I had finally found the woman I wanted to spend the rest of my life with. Instead, I just managed to be another notch in her bed post," he hissed.

"Max—" she whispered, but he cut her off.

"You never talk about anything! You let it build until your body breaks down. I actually know very little about you. You were raised on a farm, and your favorite color is blue. That's not really a lot," Max yelled.

Stiffening her spine, she said, "I don't like blue; I look good in blue. My favorite color is orange, but I cannot wear it. I wear heels because I am short, and nobody takes me seriously when I'm the height of a ten-year-old."

"Why don't you wear shorts?" he asked.

"They make my legs look stubby. I would rather be hot than stubby looking." She admitted.

"What happened to your mom?"

"She left when I was twelve, and I never saw her again. It destroyed my family. We were never the same again."

"Why didn't you ever talk to anyone at Rodgers?" he asked.

"Because I was immature when I started, and I wasn't comfortable there. I thought one day I would be, but I never was. I was good at my job, but I sucked at being interpersonal." She didn't turn around.

"When did we meet for the first time?" He already knew the answer.

"Eight in the morning on Monday, May 13. You were in the elevator talking to Grant about how you weren't nervous about the job," she said. "I found out your name within the hour. Your last name was Valentine, and your hair looked like melted dark chocolate. Your eyes were gray, and I had never met a person with gray eyes before. You shook my hand, but you were looking at Faith Nelson and not me."

"You don't know how much I wish I could go back and look you in the eyes. I missed ten years with you for no reason," Max replied, shaking his head.

"When did you first meet me?" Della asked.

"I knew you. You worked next door and had all the answers. I hated that you knew so much and that you were rarely stumped on a case. The first time I ever wanted to be your friend was in the bar after you got fired. I saw the real you for the first time that night. I was shocked when I found you at the farmer's market. I was going to go back and find you the next week," Max answered honestly.

She gave no indication that she heard what he'd said. Her back was still to him, and her arms were wrapped around her body. The dress clung to her, and her hair was starting to escape the bun on her head.

"Why don't you sleep?" he asked, quieter this time.

"My body doesn't need as much as yours; it never has. Usually, I get four or five hours. Once I wake up, I can't sleep again, so I don't try anymore."

Max looked at her. "What did your father do that was unforgivable?"

"He … he wasn't there when I needed him the most. He left me alone to face the worst day of my life alone."

"What was the worst day of your life?" he asked, wanting to touch her, but not daring.

Max knew she wasn't going to answer. He had asked too much. Della took a deep breath and said, "The worst day of my life was the day I put my newborn baby up for adoption."

He pulled her into his arms. He hadn't known what she was going to say, but that had to be the last thing he'd expected.

"That was also the day I had a hysterectomy, so I would never have another one." Her head fell forward, but she didn't pull away from him.

"I'm sorry, Della. I am so sorry that your dad wasn't there for you," he whispered into her ear.

"He only came the next day to make sure I signed the papers. He wasn't there when I had her or when I came out of surgery afterwards. I was in the hospital alone for four more days before I was discharged. I took a taxi to my apartment," she sobbed, her words were ragged as she told him.

"How old were you?" Max needed to know.

"I had her on my sixteenth birthday. I went to a party during the fall of my freshman year. I drank too much—I still don't drink because of it. I don't remember anything about that night."

Max closed his eyes and smoothed a hand over her hair. "I'm am so sorry, Della."

"Now you know that I'm not worth your time. I can't give you the babies you want. I can't have kids, Max. I can't have your babies," she said, so quietly he barely heard her, but he felt her pulling away from him.

Holding her tight to him he answered, "I don't need babies, Della. I need you."

He felt a tear hit his arm. "You need better than me. I'm not worth it."

"Worth it or not, Della Hart, I love you. I've been lost without you. I haven't been able to do anything but come up with ways to get you back. But I had no idea what I had done, so making it right was impossible." He slowly turned her in his arms so that they were facing each other.

"I haven't been doing so hot without you either," she admitted, wiping away her tears.

"You look pretty hot to me, he said, sliding his hands into her hair and touching his forehead to hers.

"Max," she warned.

"Della, you are going to have to get used to me complementing you. I'm going to do it forever," he whispered.

"Don't make promises you can't keep, Max Valentine."

"Why do you always call me Max Valentine, not just Max?" he asked.

She blushed before she answered. "Because I've had a crush on Max Valentine for years, and crushes always have two names."

"What about the man you love? What do you call him?"

Della smiled shyly, then peeked up at him through her lashes. "I've always called him Max Valentine. I can't change now."

Laughing, he took her face in his hands to kiss the crazy woman he loved, but her phone rang before he could. Looking at it, she said, "I have to answer this."

Letting her go was hard. He finally had her back in his arms. He watched her back as she talked, or rather listened to the person on the other end. Was it another client with an emergency? Was it one of her sisters?

When the call ended, she lowered the phone and turned back to him. "They're predicting that I'm going to win. There are only two precincts that aren't in, but I don't need to win them to win the election. Max … I'm a judge."

"I told you that you would win, Judge Hart," he said with a smile.

"Judge *Connor Hart*," she corrected him. Within four steps, he had her in his arms again, spinning her around in circles as she laughed. "Oh god, I can't laugh today! Mae died."

Slowly, he put her down and replied, "Mae wanted you to win. She voted for you."

"I know, it's just that—" her words stopped when she heard voices headings towards them.

Looking up, Max saw her sisters and their husbands walking down the hall. They were dressed up as well, dresses, suits, and all. "Your sisters are here."

"I know." Then she pulled out of his arms but didn't let go of him. She just waited for them to come down the hallway.

That's when he saw two little girls pull away from Zoey and run down the hallway towards them. They were about the same size with brown hair and blue dresses. He couldn't remember them from the summer. Turning to ask Della, he saw she had crouched down and had her arms out as the little girls plowed into her.

As he watched the woman he loved hug the two little girls, Max wondered what he'd missed. The taller one pulled away from Della and said, "Mommy Della, Zoey said that Mae is in heaven like Mommy. Is that true?"

Della stroked the girls' heads as she said, "Yes. Mae is keeping your mommy company in heaven. You know how Mae likes visitors."

She hugged the girls again and turned to look at Max. "Max, this is Molly and Lily. They were Beth's girls, but they want me to be their mommy now."

The news hit Max hard. Kids. A few months later, and she had kids. Does he even want kids? Looking down at the three of them, he realized that he loved her with the girls gathered in her arms just as much as before.

Max sank to his knees to be at their level and stuck his hand out to the closest to him. "Are you Molly or Lily?"

The little girl sitting on Della's knee pointed to herself and said, "I'm Molly. She's Lily."

"Well, Molly, it's nice to meet you. I think that we're going to have to get to know each other. I think your mommy Della wants me to move in with you guys," he said to the kids. He watched them snuggle into Della's arms. "Did you not just tell me you can't have kids? Now you have two."

"These two came as a surprise to me a few months ago, and it was an opportunity I couldn't pass up. I'm sorry, Max, but we're a package deal. I understand if you don't want any of it."

Carefully, he leaned over the kids and kissed her on the mouth. "I want it all, Della Hart, as long as you are a part of it."

It was then that he realized that her entire family was watching and listening to everything that was said. Standing up, he held his hand out to help Della to her feet. Both kids wanted her to hold them, so he picked one up. Admittedly, he didn't know which one. Della picked up the other, and Max pulled her to him with one arm and faced the group.

"I have an announcement to make. I would like to introduce for the first time, Judge Delphinea Connor Hart. She won!" His words were lost in loud cheers and babies suddenly crying at the noise.

Smiling, he turned back to Della, who was smiling at him. She said in his ear, "I love you, Max Valentine."

He smiled back at her and replied, "Not as much as I love you, Della."

EPILOGUE

THE CLOCK READ 4:00 a.m. when Della woke from her slumber. It was the first day of the new year. She felt the familiar heat of Max's body behind hers, his arm holding her close to him even in sleep. Slowly, she lifted his arm and slid out from under it.

Sitting on the edge of the bed she looked down at his sleeping face. He was still gorgeous, even with his hair pointing in every direction. She wanted to touch his face but didn't because that usually woke him up. It was too early for him to get up unless she didn't want to get anything done this morning. Some mornings that was okay, but not today.

Getting up, she left the bedroom that they shared every night. They had actually gotten married a week after Mae's funeral. It had been a simple ceremony in the ballroom, but it had been all she'd needed. Now he was hers. Now she was Mrs. Max Valentine, if only at home. At work, she was Judge Della Connor Hart and had been for a year now.

Sally was now happily moved into the retirement home on the outskirts of town. Though she missed Mae terribly, she was enjoying the company of the other residents. When she had been asked, she had willingly agreed to move out of the big old house. It had been Mae's home, not hers for all those years. They went and visited her once or twice a week.

The house next door that Max had inherited sat mostly empty, and neither of them dreamed of moving across the street with their little family. Every once in a while, his sisters or mother would come to stay for a few days. Sometimes an old friend would come and stay for a while, but starting this summer, Max was going to run it as a bed and breakfast to see if he can get people to come to town. Her Max Valentine was full of ideas.

Quietly, she opened the door down the hallway, one of the many empty ones when she first moved in, and peaked her head in. Both girls were still sleeping. Della smiled at their sleeping forms, her babies. Both had excepted Max as if he'd been there the entire time. It had only taken three days for Molly to run to him instead of Della when she was excited or scared. At first it had hurt Della's feelings to be replaced so quickly, but she would've happened eventually—everybody loves Max Valentine.

Max had turned into a marvelous father. Though he had been nervous at first, within a week, he was crawling around the floor with the girls and carrying them on his shoulders. That had been almost fourteen months ago, and they were his shadows now.

Leaving the door open so she could hear them when they woke up, Della quietly went into her office, now the family room. Her sanctuary had been overtaken by dozens of toys. Picking up a few, she couldn't stop smiling as she put them in the toy box in the corner.

The last year had been amazing. Even though they had gotten married before the year had started, the adoption had been finalized in May, but the adoption was only paperwork. They had been a family since that November night. Max had moved to Birch Cove and into her house within days. He had never left. He had never even talked about it.

Earlier that year, Max had published his first book. Della had read it and surprised to see it was beautifully written. The topic wasn't her favorite, but she'd read it because he wrote it. He had started a new book, but it was slower to write when you have two little kids demanding your attention, but Max wouldn't have it any other way.

There was practically a baby boom within the people she loved the most. Nathan and Diana had started it by having a girl in July. Zoey and Gabe had another boy in October, making Della work the Pumpkin Patch another year. But this time, she got to bring her girls to spend time on the farm she had grown up on. Lea and Casey had married and were due any day now. Their two girls were excited for a baby in the house. Then, if Della had noticed correctly last Christmas, Evie would be announcing another Reed baby soon.

Della grabbed her laptop and turned it on. While waiting for it to come to life, she walked over to the bookcase. Reaching for the top shelf, she pulled down an envelope, then brought it over to the couch and opened it again. All it contained was a letter and an old picture. Over the last few months, she had memorized the letter and the picture, but she had to hold them sometimes.

The smiling fourteen-year-old in the picture had long black hair with large, wavy curls. The eyes looking back at her were her green ones, and they were happy. To Della, she seemed caught in the laugh. Every time she looked at it, she tried to see herself in the girl's features, but there were only the curls and the green eyes. The letter told of her wonderful life and great parents. It thanked her for letting her parents adopt her because they needed her in their lives. They had kept her name as Natalie. Della knew the picture was old, her daughter was nineteen now, but it was something she could see and touch.

She had received the envelope the second week in January a year ago. She had cried as she looked at the picture and read the information. She had quickly sent off another letter but never heard back again. But at least now she knew her daughter was happy. So far, she had only shown Max the picture and the letter; this was hers for now. She wasn't ready to share Natalie with her sisters yet.

Seeing that the computer was up, Della stood and put the envelope away. She would probably look at again tomorrow; she usually started her day looking at it. After sitting back on the couch, she pulled the computer onto her lap and smiled at the screen saver. It was of her and her sisters. It had been taken years ago when Zoey had first came home, and they had come down to bring Della's car back after Zoey had driven it home. Della had never told them that it had taken her over two hours to get to work that week. Evie was still Evie with her long hair, which had grown back after she'd cut it two years ago. Zoey had her bouncy, crazy curls. Della had her mousy brown hair. Touching her red curls now, she was glad she made the change. They had their arms around each other and were smiling for the camera.

Della loved this photo. Even though none of them looked good in the picture, it reminded her of all that had happened in their lives since then. Love, marriage, kids, houses, jobs … they had been through a lot. And it seemed that the Hart sisters had finally been able to find happiness.

WHO IS IN THE PICTURE???

Brian Wainwright,

Thank you for informing me that Catherine has passed and that she didn't suffer. Though our marriage has been long over, I still feel for the woman and didn't wish her dead.

You mentioned in your letter that Catherine had a child, a twelve-year-old girl. I knew that Catherine was pregnant the last time we spoke. But she knew then, and I will tell you also, the child is not my responsibility. That is all Catherine.

If my name is listed on the birth certificate or in any legal document, I request that it be removed as soon as possible. I am in no way a father to that child, and no amount of paperwork will change that. I have enclosed a document that I had drawn up that severs any legal connection I may have to the mentioned child. She is not mine, and she is not my concern.

I have spent years raising the children Catherine left behind, and they are now adults. I am done with that responsibility. I don't want or need another one of her mistakes in my life. The ones I raised were enough for this lifetime.

Please kindly inform the girl that I wish her no harm, but I in no way want her in my life. You mentioned that without me, she would end up in foster care. I know you mentioned this to make me reconsider, but it didn't work. The girl has no home here and never will.

Charlie Hart

Brian reread the letter that was sending an innocent twelve-year-old into the system. A system that was unforgiving and cruel. As a cop of thirty years, he had seen the results of foster care first-hand.

He wondered why the man hadn't returned the picture he had sent. Had it been forgotten, or had the girl sparked something in a bitter man who didn't deserve this little girl in life anyway. Brian felt sorry for the children that he had already raised.

Brian looked up at the mentioned twelve-year-old, who was sitting in the uncomfortable chair across from his desk. Her curly hair was tied in a ponytail that need some help from someone who cared. But this girl was now an orphan in the system, and there would be nobody to help her again. From here on out, she was on her own.

"He doesn't want me?" Zephyr Hart nodded at the letter. At twelve, she didn't act like a kid, but a world-wary adult trapped in a youthful body.

"That's what is says." He couldn't not tell her. Though the exact content of the letter, he would keep to himself.

"I told you their relationship ended badly." Echoing the letter, she crossed her arms over the oversized sweatshirt even though it was over eighty degrees and humid outside. She was in a sweatshirt and long pants, and her feet were encased in tennis shoes so old that he knew she wasn't the first owner.

"And you are twelve, so I decided I needed to hear that from your dad." He admitted she had told him that, a month before when he had sent the letter. Brian had taken an interest in her case since he had been the one who had informed her that her mother had died.

"He isn't my dad."

"Your birth certificate says he is."

"Dads love their kids. Charlie Hart doesn't even think about me. Never has."

"Did you want me to contact your sisters? In the document, your dad, Charlie, requested to remove his three children from responsibly for you also. But they are grown women, and they can make that discussion for themselves."

Zephyr's foot swung as she thought about it, her blue eyes looking off at some spot beyond his left ear. For a kid, she was a deep-thinker, always taking more time than most to come up with her answer.

"No, I'll go into foster care. They don't want me." Crumpling the letter, he knew the kid had been dealt a blow with the parents that she had been given. Neither deserved her, and now neither would have her.

"They might not know about you."

"They have each other, and they are 'the girls.' Let's leave them happy." Her words hurt him because he knew she believed them. Zephyr believed that with her, they couldn't or wouldn't be happy.

"Are you sure, Zephyr? You don't know them. How do you know they won't want you?"

"Mom didn't want me there, so I will stay here." The woman didn't deserve to die the way she had, but she also wasn't the parent this girl had needed.

"I can keep pursuing this." His mind started looking for the sisters who were adults and could take a child on. Unless she was right and they didn't want her … then what? Disappoint the kid again?

"No, I will be fine. I always have been before," she assured him as she gathered up her notebooks from the chair beside her. They were just cheap notebooks, mostly dog-eared and something she always carried with her. Today was no exception to that. Not once had she told him what was in them, and he hadn't dared ask her.

With the letter still in his hand, he knew he wanted to adopt this girl. She needed someone, and he wanted to be that someone, someone who wanted and loved her just for who she was. His adopted son was an adult now and had joined the marines, which left his spare bedroom empty. It seemed the timing was perfect and so was the kid, because he loved this kid despite himself. Just like his son.

At this point, he didn't see anything that would stand in the way of him adopting her. Not a thing stood in their way of being a family.

Find out what happened to Zephyr Hart in Keeping Her Safe.

ALSO BY ALIE GARNETT

<u>Indulge</u>

Craving Winter

Enticing Aurora

<u>Landstad, ND</u>

Invisible

Irresistible

Impulsive

Insuppressible

Intriguing

Imperfect

Irreplaceable

<u>The Great Lovely Falls</u>

Falling for the Single Mom

Falling for his Best Friends Sister

Falling for the Boss

Falling for his Step-Sister

Falling for his Fake Wife

Falling into a Second Chance

<u>Hart Series</u>

Seeing her Pain

Her Favor

Max Valentine is Looking at Me!

Keeping her Safe

<u>Stand Alone</u>

Romancing the Doctor

ABOUT ME, ALIE GARNETT

I love to read and prefer a little spice in those books. I am lucky enough to live on a small hobby farm in northern Minnesota with her husband and two kids. I enjoy spending time in the pasture with my two mini horses and one fainting goat (who doesn't actually faint). When I'm not writing, I'm busy trying to do all the things I didn't get to while writing. Or maybe I wouldn't have gotten to them anyway, because its laundry, dishes and fun things like that.